U0927081

# 原来你也在这里

Here Art Thou

## 泰戈尔最美的100首诗

[印]罗宾德拉纳特·泰戈尔 Rabindranath Tagore /著

郑振铎 冰心/译

CNS 湖南文艺出版社 HUNAN LITERATURE AND ART PUBLISHING HOUSE 博集天卷 CS-BOOKY

# 目录

# Contents

生如夏花 001

002 · 献歌 · 生命

055 · 永恒 · 时光

096 · 真与幻 · 爱情

139 · 短而长 · 旅途

176 · 孩子 · 天使

附录 

太戈尔传

# 生如夏花

原来你也在这里

HERE ART THOU

# 献歌·生命

使生如夏花之绚烂，死如秋叶之静美。

——《飞鸟集》八二 郑振铎 译 一九二二年六月——

Let life be beautiful like summer flowers and death like autumn leaves.

我旅行的时间很长，旅途也是很长的。

天刚破晓，我就驱车起行，穿遍广漠的世界，在许多星球之上，留下辙痕。

离你最近的地方，路途最远，最简单的音调，需要最艰苦的练习。

旅客要在每一个生人门口敲叩，才能敲到自己的家门，人要在外面到处漂流，最后才能走到最深的内殿。

我的眼睛向空阔处四望，最后才合上眼说“你原来在

这里！”

这句问话和呼唤“呵，在哪儿呢？”融化在千股的泪泉里，和你保证的回答“我在这里！”的洪流，一同泛滥了全世界。

——《吉檀迦利》一二 冰心译 一九五五年四月——

The time that my journey takes is long and the way of it long.

I came out on the chariot of the first gleam of light, and pursued my voyage through the wildernesses of worlds leaving my track on many a star and planet.

It is the most distant course that comes nearest to thyself, and that training is the most intricate which leads to the utter simplicity of a tune.

The traveller has to knock at every alien door to come to his own, and one has to wander through all the outer worlds to reach the innermost shrine at the end.

My eyes strayed far and wide before I shut them and said “Here art thou!”

The question and the cry “Oh, where?” melt into tears of a thousand streams and deluge the world with the flood of the assurance “I am!”

你为什么这样低声地对我耳语，呵，“死亡”，我的“死亡”？

当花儿晚谢，牛儿归棚，你偷偷地走到我身边，说出我不了解的话语。

难道你必须用昏沉的微语和冰冷的接吻，来向我求爱来赢得我心么，呵，“死亡”，我的“死亡”？

我们的婚礼不会有铺张的仪式吗？

在你褐黄的鬈发上不系上花串吗？

在你前面没有举旗的人么？你也没有通红的火炬，使黑夜像着火一样地明亮么，呵，“死亡”，我的“死亡”？

你吹着法螺来吧，在无眠之夜来吧。

给我穿上红衣，紧握我的手把我娶走吧。

让你的驾着急躁嘶叫的马的车辇，准备好等在我门前吧。

揭开我的面纱骄傲地看我的脸吧，呵，“死亡”，我的“死亡”！

——《园丁集》八一 冰心 译 一九五八年五月《泰戈尔诗选》——

Why do you whisper so faintly in my ears, O Death, my Death?

When the flowers droop in the evening and cattle come back to their stalls, you stealthily come to my side and speak words that I do not understand.

Is this how you must woo and win me, with the opiate of drowsy murmur and cold kisses, O Death, my Death?

Will there be no proud ceremony for our wedding?

Will you not tie up with a wreath your tawny coiled locks?

Is there none to carry your banner before you, and will not the night be on fire with your red torch-lights, O Death, my Death?

Come with your conch-shells sounding, come in the sleepless night.

Dress me with a crimson mantle, grasp my hand and take me.

Let your chariot be ready at my door with your horses neighing impatiently.

Raise my veil and look at my face proudly, O Death, my Death!

我今晨坐在窗前，“世界”如一个过路人似的，停留了一会，向我点点头又走去了。

——《飞鸟集》一六 郑振铎 译 一九二二年六月——

I sit at my window this morning where the world like a passer-by stops for a moment, nods to me and goes.

我每天把纸船一个个放在急流的溪中。

我用大黑字写我的名字和我住的地名在纸船上。

我希望住在异地的人得到了这纸船，就知道我是谁。

我把园中长的希利花载在这些小船上，希望这些黎明开的花能在夜里平平安安地带到岸上。

我投我的纸船到水里，仰看天空，看见小朵的云正张着满鼓着风的白帆。

我不知道是不是天上的游伴把这些船放下来同我的船比赛!

夜来了，我的脸埋在手臂里，梦见我的纸船在中夜的星辰下面渐渐的浮泛上去。

“睡之仙人”坐在船里，带着他们满载着梦的篮子。

——《新月集·纸船》郑振铎 译　一九二三年九月——

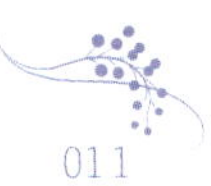

## PAPER BOATS

Day by day I float my paper boats one by one down the running stream.

In big black letters I write my name on them and the name of the village where I live.

I hope that someone in some strange land will find them and know who I am.

I load my little boats with shiuli flowers from our garden, and hope that these blooms of the dawn will be carried safely to land in the night.

I launch my paper boats and look up into the sky and see the little clouds setting their white bulging sails.

I know not what playmate of mine in the sky sends them down the air to race with my boats!

When night comes I bury my face in my arms and dream that my paper boats float on and on under the midnight stars.

The fairies of sleep are sailing in them, and the lading is their baskets full of dreams.

我少年时候的生命如同一朵花一般——当春天的微飔来求乞于她的门上时，一朵花从她的丰富里失去一两瓣花片也并不觉得损失。

现在少年的光阴过去了，我的生命如同一个果子一般，没有什么东西耗费了，只等着完完全全地带着她的充实甜美的负担，贡献她自己。

——《采果集》二 郑振铎 译

二〇〇九年六月，北京十月文艺出版社《新月集·飞鸟集》——

My life when young was like a flower——a flower that loosens a petal or two from her abundance and never feels the loss when the spring breeze comes to beg at her door.

Now at the end of youth my life is like a fruit,having nothing to spare, and  waiting to offer herself completely with her full burden of sweetness.

这是我对你的祈求，我的主——请你铲除，铲除我心里贫乏的根源。

赐给我力量使我能轻闲地承受欢乐与忧伤。

赐给我力量使我的爱在服务中得到果实。

赐给我力量使我永不抛弃穷人也永不向淫威屈膝。

赐给我力量使我的心灵超越于日常琐事之上。

再赐给我力量使我满怀爱意地把我的力量服从你意志的指挥。

——《吉檀迦利》三六 冰心 译 一九五五年四月——

This is my prayer to thee, my lord—strike, strike at the root of penury in my heart.

Give me the strength lightly to bear my joys and sorrows.

Give me the strength to make my love fruitful in service.

Give me the strength never to disown the poor or bend my knees before insolent might.

Give me the strength to raise my mind high above daily trifles.

And give me the strength to surrender my strength to thy will with love.

我的思想随着这些闪耀的绿叶而闪耀着，我的心灵触着这日光也唱了起来，我的生命因为偕了万物一同浮泛在空间的蔚蓝，时间的墨黑中，正在快乐着呢。

——《飞鸟集》一五〇 郑振铎 译 一九二二年六月——

My thoughts shimmer with these shimmering leaves and my heart sings with the touch of this sunlight; my life is glad to be floating with all things into the blue of space, into the dark of time.

你已经使我永生，这样做是你的欢乐。这脆薄的杯儿，你不断的把它倒空，又不断的以新生命来充满。

这小小的苇笛，你携带着它逾山越谷，从笛管里吹出永新的音乐。

在你双手的不朽的按抚下，我的小小的心，消融在无边快乐之中，发出不可言说的词调。

你的无穷的赐予只倾入我小小的手里。时代过去了，你还在倾注，而我的手里还有余量待充满。

——《吉檀迦利》一　冰心译　一九五五年四月——

Thou hast made me endless, such is thy pleasure. This frail vessel thou emptiest again and again, and fillest it ever with fresh life.

This little flute of a reed thou hast carried over hills and dales, and hast breathed through it melodies eternally new.

At the immortal touch of thy hands my little heart loses its limits in joy and gives birth to utterance ineffable.

Thy infinite gifts come to me only on these very small hands of mine. Ages pass, and still thou pourest, and still there is room to fill.

我常常思索，人和动物之间没有语言，他们心中互相认识的界线在哪里。

在远古创世的清晨，通过哪一条太初乐园的单纯的小径，他们的心曾彼此访问过。

他们的亲属关系早被忘却，他们不变的足印的符号并没有消灭。

可是忽然在那无言的音乐中，那模糊的记忆清醒起来，动物用温柔的信任注视着人的脸，人也用嘻嬉笑的感情下望着它的眼睛。

好像两个朋友戴着面具相逢，在伪装下彼此模糊地互认着。

——《园丁集》七九 冰心 译 一九五八年五月《泰戈尔诗选》——

I often wonder where lie hidden the boundaries of recognition between man and the beast whose heart knows no spoken language.

Through what primal paradise in a remote morning of creation ran the simple path by which their hearts visited each other?

Those marks of their constant tread have not been effaced though their kinship has been long forgotten.

Yet suddenly in some wordless music the dim memory wakes up and the beast gazes into the man's face with a tender trust, and the man looks down into its eyes with amused affection.

It seems that the two friends meet masked and vaguely know each other through the disguise.

世界对了他的爱人，把他朦朦的面具揭下了。

他变小了，小如一首歌，小如一回永久的接吻。

——《飞鸟集》三 郑振铎 译 一九二二年六月——

The world puts off its mask of vastness to its lover. It becomes small as one song, as one kiss of the eternal.

“呵，诗人，夜晚渐临；你的头发已经变白。

“在你孤寂的沉思中听到了来生的消息么？”

“是夜晚了，”诗人说，“夜虽已晚，我还在静听，因为也许有人会从村中呼唤。

“我看守着，是否有年轻的飘游的心聚在一起，两对渴望的眼睛切盼有音乐来打破他们的沉默，并替他们说话。

“如果我坐在生命的岸边默想着死亡和来世，又有谁来编写他们的热情的诗歌呢？

“早现的晚星消隐了。

“火葬灰中的红光在沉静的河边慢慢地熄灭下去。

“残月的微光下，胡狼从空宅的庭院里齐声嗥叫。

“假如有游子们离了家，到这里来守夜，低头静听黑暗的微语，有谁把生命的秘密向他耳边低诉呢，如果我关起门户，企图摆脱世俗的牵缠？

“我的头发变白是一件小事。

“我是永远和这村里最年轻的人一样的年轻，最年老的人一样的年老。

“有的人发出甜柔单纯的微笑，有的人眼里含着狡狯的闪光。

“有的人在白天流涌着眼泪，有的人的眼泪却隐藏在幽暗里。

“他们都需要我，我没有时间去冥想来生。

“我和每一个人都是同年的，我的头发变白了又该怎样呢？”

——《园丁集》二 冰心 译 一九五八年五月《泰戈尔诗选》——

"Ah, poet, the evening draws near; your hair is turning grey.

"Do you in your lonely musing hear the message of the hereafter?"

"It is evening," the poet said, "and I am listening because some one may call from the village, late though it be.

"I watch if young straying hearts meet together and two pairs of eager eyes beg for music to break their silence and speak for them.

"Who is there to weave their passionate songs, if I sit on the shore of life and contemplate death and the beyond?

"The early evening star disappears.

"The glow of a funeral pyre slowly dies by the slient river.

"Jackals cry in chorus from the courtyard of the deserted house in the light of the worn-out moon.

"If some wanderer leaving home, come here to watch the night and with bowed head listen to the murmur of the darkness, who is there to whisper the secrets of life into his ears if I, shutting my doors, should try to free myself from mortal bonds?

"It is a trifle that my hair is turning grey.

"I am ever as young or as old as the youngest and the oldest of this village.

"Some have smiles, sweet and simple, and some a sly twinkle in their eyes.

"Some have tears that well up in the daylight, and others tears that are hidden in the gloom.

"They all have need for me and I have no time to brood over the afterlife.

"I am of an age with each, what matter if my hair turns grey?"

夏天的飞鸟，飞到我窗前唱歌，又飞去了。

秋天的黄叶，他们没有什么可唱，只叹息一声，飞落在那里。

——《飞鸟集》一 郑振铎 译 一九二二年六月——

Stray birds of summer come to my window to sing and fly away. And yellow leaves of autumn, which have no songs, flutter and fall there with a sigh.

请容我懈怠一会儿，来坐在你的身旁。我手边的工作等一下再去完成。

不在你的面前，我的心就不知道什么是安逸和休息，我的工作变成了无边的劳役海中的无尽的劳役。

今天，炎暑来到我的窗前，轻嘘微语；群蜂在花树的宫廷中尽情弹唱。

这正是应该静坐的时光，和你相对，在这静寂和无边的闲暇里唱出生命的献歌。

——《吉檀迦利》五　冰心　译　一九五五年四月——

I ask for a moment's indulgence to sit by thy side. The works that I have in hand I will finish afterwards.

Away from the sight of thy face my heart knows no rest nor respite, and my work becomes an endless toil in a shoreless sea of toil.

Today the summer has come at my window with its sighs and murmurs; and the bees are playing their minstrelsy at the court of the flowering grove.

Now it is time to sit quiet, face to face with thee, and to sing dedication of life in this silent and overflowing leisure.

呵，疯狂的、头号的醉汉；
如果你踢开门户在大众面前装疯；
如果你在一夜倒空囊橐，对慎重轻蔑地弹着指头；
如果你走着奇怪的道路，和无益的东西游戏；
不理会韵律和理性；
如果你在风暴前扯起船帆，你把船舵折成两半，
那么我就要跟随你，伙伴，喝得烂醉走向堕落灭亡。

我在稳重聪明的街坊中间虚度了日日夜夜。
过多的知识使我白了头发，过多的观察使我眼力模糊。
多年来我积攒了许多零碎的东西：
把这些东西摔碎，在上面跳舞，把它们散掷到风中去吧。
因为我知道喝得烂醉而堕落灭亡，是最高的智慧。

让一切歪曲的顾虑消亡吧，让我无望地迷失了路途。
让一阵旋风吹来，把我连船锚一齐卷走。
世界上住着高尚的人，劳动的人，有用又聪明。
有的人很从容地走在前头，有的人庄重地走在后面。

让他们快乐繁荣吧，让我傻呆地无用吧。

因为我知道喝得烂醉而堕落灭亡，是一切工作的结局。

我此刻誓将一切的要求，让给正人君子。

我抛弃我学识的自豪和是非的判断。

我打碎记忆的瓶壶，挥洒最后的眼泪。

以红果酒的泡沫来洗澡，使我欢笑发出光辉。

我暂且撕裂温恭和认真的标志。

我将发誓作一个无用的人，喝得烂醉而堕落灭亡下去。

——《园丁集》四二 冰心 译 一九五八年五月《泰戈尔诗选》——

O mad, superbly drunk;

If you kick open your doors and play the fool in public;

If you empty your bag in a night, and snap your fingers at prudence;

If you walk in curious paths and play with useless things;

Reck not rhyme or reason;

If unfurling your sails before the storm you snap the rudder in two,

Then I will follow you, comrade, and be drunken and go to the dogs.

I have wasted my days and nights in the company of steady wise neighbours.

Much knowing has turned my hair grey, and much watching has made my sight dim.

For years I have gathered and heaped up scraps and fragments of things:

Crush them and dance upon them, and scatter them all to the winds.

For I know it is the height of wisdom to be drunken and go to the dogs.

Let all crooked scruples vanish, let me hopelessly lose

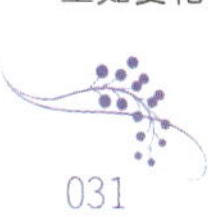

my way.

Let a gust of wild giddiness come and sweep me away from my anchors.

The world is peopled with worthies, and workers, useful and clever.

There are men who are easily first, and men who come decently after.

Let them be happy and prosper, and let me be foolishly futile.

For I know it is the end of all works to be drunken and go to the dogs.

I swear to surrender this moment all claims to the ranks of the decent.

I let go my pride of learning and judgment of right and of wrong.

I'll shatter memory's vessel, scattering the last drop of tears.

With the foam of the berry-red wine I will bathe and brighten my laughter.

The badge of the civil and staid I'll tear into shreds for the nonce.

I'll take the holy vow to be worthless, to be drunken and go to the dogs.

“海水呀，你说的什么？”

“是永久的疑问。”

“天空呀，你怎么回答？”[1]

“是永久的沉默。”

——《飞鸟集》一二 郑振铎 译 一九二二年六月——

“What language is thine, O sea?”
“The language of eternal question.”
“What language is thy answer, O sky?”
“The language of eternal silence.”

①郑振铎《飞鸟集》附录中改为“你回答的话是什么？”

对那些定要离开的客人们，求神帮他们快走，并且扫掉他们所有的足迹。

把舒服的单纯的亲近的，微笑着一起抱在你的怀里。

今天是幻影的节日，他们不知道自己的死期。

让你的笑声只作为无意义的欢乐，像浪花上的闪光。

让你的生命像露珠在叶尖一样，在时间的边缘上轻轻跳舞。

在你的琴弦上弹出无定的暂时的音调吧。

——《园丁集》四五 冰心 译 一九五八年五月《泰戈尔诗选》——

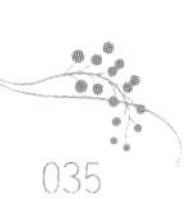



To the guests that must go bid God's speed and brush away all traces of their steps.

Take to your bosom with a smile what is easy and simple and near.

To-day is the festival of phantoms that know not when they die.

Let your laughter be but a meaningless mirth like twinkles of light on the ripples.

Let your life lightly dance on the edges of Time like dew on the tip of a leaf.

Strike in chords from your harp fitful momentary rhythms.

早晨，我在石铺的路上走时，我叫道，“来雇我。”

皇帝坐着马车，手里拿着剑走来。

他拿住我的手，说道，“我要用权力来雇你。”

但是他的权力算不了什么，他坐着马车走了。

正午炎热的时候，家家的门都闭着。

我沿着屈曲的小道走去。

一个老人带着一袋金钱走出来。

他斟酌了一下，说道，“我要用金钱来雇你。”

他一个一个地称量他的钱，但我却转身离去了。

黄昏的时候，花园的篱上满开着花。

美人走出来，说道，“我要用微笑来雇你。”

她的微笑灰白了，融化成眼泪了，她孤寂地回身走进黑暗里去。

太阳照耀在沙土上，海波刚愎地碎开了。

一个小孩坐在那里，拿贝壳做游戏。

他抬起头来，好像认识我似的，说道，“我雇你不用什么东西。”

这个小孩的游戏中的买卖，使我从此以后，成了一个自由的人。

——《新月集·最后的契约》郑振铎 译 一九二三年九月——

## THE LAST BARGAIN

“Come and hire me,” I cried, while in the morning I was walking on the stonepaved road.

Sword in hand, the King came in his chariot.

He held my hand and said, “I will hire you with my power.”

But his power counted for nought, and he went away in his chariot.

In the heat of the midday the houses stood with shut doors.

I wandered along the crooked lane.

An old man came out with his bag of gold.

He pondered and said, “I will hire you with my money.”

He weighed his coin one by one, but I turned away.

It was evening. The garden hedge was all flower.

The fair maid came out and said, “I will hire you with a smile.”

Her smile paled and melted into tears, and she went back alone into the dark.

The sun glistened on the sand, and the sea waves broke waywardly.

A child sat playing with shells.

He raised his head and seemed to know me, and said, “I hire you with nothing.”

From thenceforward that bargain struck in child's play made me a free man.

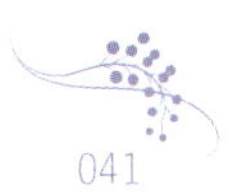



无量的财富不是你的，我的耐心的微黑的尘土母亲。

你操劳着来填满你孩子们的嘴，但是粮食是很少的。

你给我们的欢乐礼物，永远不是完全的。

你给你孩子们做的玩具，是不牢的。

你不能满足我们的一切渴望，但是我能为此就背弃你么?

你的含着痛苦阴影的微笑，对我的眼睛是甜柔的。

你的永不满足的爱，对我的心是亲切的。

从你的胸乳里，你是以生命而不是以不朽来哺育我们，因此你的眼睛永远是警醒的。

累年积代地你用颜色和诗歌来工作，但是你的天堂还没有盖起，仅有天堂的愁苦的意味。

你的美的创造上蒙着泪雾。

我将把我的诗歌倾注入你无言的心里，把我的爱倾注入你的爱中。

我将用劳动来礼拜你。

我看见过你的温慈的面庞，我爱你的悲哀的尘土，大地母亲。

——《园丁集》七三 冰心 译 一九五八年五月《泰戈尔诗选》——

Infinite wealth is not yours, my patient and dusky mother dust!

You toil to fill the mouths of your children, but food is scarce.

The gift of gladness that you have for us is never perfect.

The toys that you make for your children are fragile.

You cannot satisfy all our hungry hopes, but should I desert you for that?

Your smile which is shadowed with pain is sweet to my eyes.

Your love which knows not fulfillment is dear to my heart.

From your breast you have fed us with life but not immortality, that is why your eyes are ever wakeful.

For ages you are working with colour and song, yet your heaven is not built, but only its sad suggestion.

Over your creations of beauty there is the mist of tears.

I will pour my songs into your mute heart, and my love into your love.

I will worship you with labour.

I have seen your tender face and I love your mournful dust, Mother Earth.

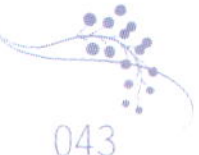

创造的神秘，有如夜时的黑暗——这是伟大的。知识的幻影，不过如晨间之雾。

——《飞鸟集》一四 郑振铎 译 一九二二年六月——

The mystery of creation is like the darkness of night–it is great. Delusions of knowledge are like the fog of the morning.

西乡来的工人和他的妻子正忙着替砖窑挖土。

他们的小女儿到河边的渡头上；她无休无歇地擦洗锅盘。

她的小弟弟，光着头，赤裸着黧黑的涂满泥土的身躯，跟着她，听她的话，在高高的河岸上耐心地等着她。

她顶着满瓶的水，平稳地走回家去，左手提着发亮的铜壶，右手拉着那个孩子——她是妈妈的小丫头，繁重的家务使她变得严肃了。

有一天我看见那赤裸的孩子伸着腿坐着。

他姐姐坐在水里，用一把土在转来转去地擦洗一把水壶。

一只毛茸茸的小羊，在河岸上吃草。

它走近这孩子身边，忽然大叫了一声，孩子吓得哭喊起来。

他姐姐放下水壶跑上岸来。

她一只手抱起弟弟，一只手抱起小羊，把她的爱抚分成两半，人类和动物的后代在慈爱的连结中合一了。

——《园丁集》七七 冰心 译 一九五八年五月《泰戈尔诗选》——

The workman and his wife from the west country are busy digging to make bricks for the kiln.

Their little daughter goes to the landing-place by the river; there she has no end of scouring and scrubbing of

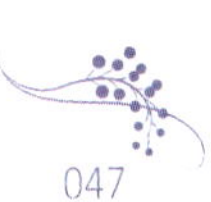

pots and pans.

Her little brother, with shaven head and brown, naked, mud-covered limbs, follows after her and waits patiently on the high bank at her bidding.

She goes back home with the full pitcher poised on her head, the shining brass pot in her left hand, holding the child with her right—she the tiny servant of her mother, grave with the weight of the household cares.

One day I saw this naked boy sitting with legs outstretched.

In the water his sister sat rubbing a drinking-pot with a handful of earth, turning it round and round.

Nearby a soft-haired lamb stood grazing along the bank.

It came close to where the boy sat and suddenly bleated aloud, and the child started up and screamed.

His sister left off cleaning her pot and ran up.

She took up her brother in one arm and the lamb in the other, and dividing her caresses between them bound in one bond of affection the offspring of beast and man.

夜与落日接吻，轻轻的在他耳旁说道，“我是死，是你的母亲。我就要给你新的生命。”

——《飞鸟集》一一九 郑振铎 译 一九二二年六月——

The night kisses the fading day whispering to his ear, “I am death, your mother. I am to give you fresh birth.”

是我走的时候了，母亲；我走了。

当清寂的黎明，你在暗中伸出双臂，要抱你睡在床上的孩子时，我要说道，“孩子不在那里呀！”——母亲，我走了。

我要变成一股清风抚摸着你，我要变成水中的小波，当你浴时把你吻了又吻。

大风之夜，当雨点在树叶中淅沥时，你在床上，会听见我的微语，当电光从开着的窗口闪进你的屋里时，我的笑声也偕了他一同闪进了。

如果你醒着躺在床上，想着你的孩子到了深夜，我便要从群星里向你唱道，“睡呀，母亲，睡呀。”

我要坐在照澈各处的月光上，偷到你的床上，乘你睡着时，躺在你的胸上。

我要变成一个梦儿，从你眼皮的小孔中，钻到你睡眠的深处；当你醒起来吃惊地四看时，我便如闪耀的萤火似的熠熠地向暗中飞去了。

当普耶大祭日①，邻家的孩子们来屋里游玩时，我便要融

①是随意指印度的某一个大祭神日。

化在笛声里，整日介在你心头震荡。

亲爱的阿姨带了普耶礼[1]来，问道："我（们）的孩子在那里呢，姊姊？"母亲，你要柔声地告诉她，"他呀，他现在是在我的瞳人里，他现在是在我的身体里，在我的灵魂里。"

——《新月集·告别》郑振铎 译 一九二三年九月——

①指某一个节日亲友相互馈送的礼物。

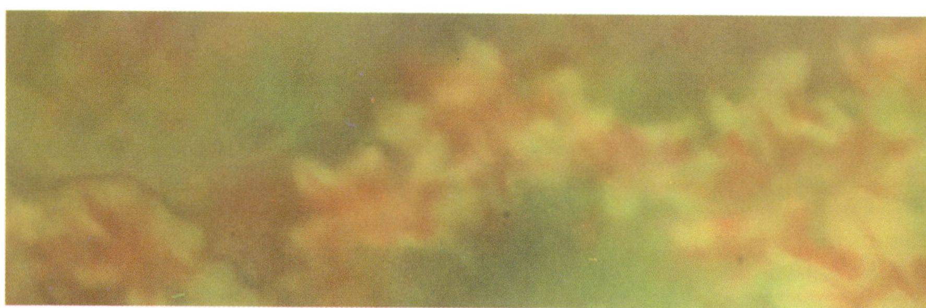

## THE END

It is time for me to go, mother; I am going.

When in the paling darkness of the lonely dawn you stretch out your arms for your baby in the bed, I shall say, "Baby is not there!"—mother, I am going.

I shall become a delicate draught of air and caress you; and I shall be ripples in the water when you bathe, and kiss you and kiss you again.

In the gusty night when the rain patters on the leaves you will hear my whisper in your bed, and my laughter will flash with the lightning through the open window into your room.

If you lie awake, thinking of your baby till late into the night, I shall sing to you from the stars, "Sleep, mother, sleep."

On the straying moonbeams I shall steal over your bed,

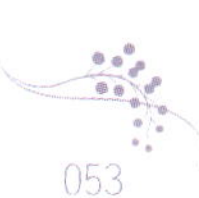

and lie upon your bosom while you sleep.

I shall become a dream, and through the little opening of your eyelids I shall slip into the depths of your sleep, and when you wake up and look round startled, like a twinkling firefly I shall flit out into the darkness.

When, on the great festival of puja, the neighbours' children come and play about the house, I shall melt into the music of the flute and throb in your heart all day.

Dear auntie will come with puja-presents and will ask, "Where is our baby, sister?" Mother, you will tell her softly, "He is in the pupils of my eyes, he is in my body and in my soul."

我们的生命就似渡过一个大海，我们都相聚在这个狭小的舟中。死时，我们便到了岸，各往各的世界去了。

——《飞鸟集》二四二 郑振铎 译 一九二二年六月——

This life is the crossing of a sea, where we meet in the same narrow ship. In death we reach the shore and go to our different worlds.

## 永恒·时光

莲花开放的那天，唉，我不自觉的在心魂飘荡。我的花篮空着，花儿我也没有去理睬。

不时的有一段幽愁来袭击我，我从梦中惊起，觉得南风里有一阵奇香的芳踪。

这迷茫的温馨，使我想望得心痛，我觉得这仿佛是夏天渴望的气息，寻求圆满。

我那时不晓得它离我是那么近，而且是我的，

这完美的温馨，还是在我自己心灵的深处开放。

——《吉檀迦利》二〇 冰心 译 一九五五年四月——

On the day when the lotus bloomed, alas, my mind was straying, and I knew it not. My basket was empty and the flower remained unheeded.

Only now and again a sadness fell upon me, and I started up from my dream and felt a sweet trace of a strange fragrance in the south wind.

That vague sweetness made my heart ache with longing and it seemed to me that it was the eager breath of the summer seeking for its completion.

I knew not then that it was so near, that it was mine, and that this perfect sweetness had blossomed in the depth of my own heart.

你是什么人，读者，百年后读着我的诗?

我不能从春天的财富里送你一朵花，从天边的云彩里送你一片金影。

开起门来四望吧。

从你的群花盛开的园子里，采取百年前消逝了的花儿的芬芳记忆。

在你心的欢乐里，愿你感到一个春晨吟唱的活的欢乐，把它快乐的声音，传过一百年的时间。

——《园丁集》八五 冰心 译 一九五八年五月《泰戈尔诗选》——

Who are you, reader, reading my poems a hundred years hence?

I cannot send you one single flower from this wealth of the spring, one single streak of gold from yonder clouds.

Open your doors and look abroad.

From your blossoming garden gather fragrant memories of the vanished flowers of a hundred years before.

In the joy of your heart may you feel the living joy that sang one spring morning, sending its glad voice across a hundred years.

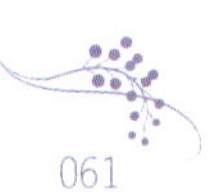



她接近我的心，如草花之接近土地；她对于我之甜蜜，如睡眠之于疲倦的肢体。我对于她的爱情是我充溢的生命的流泛，如河水之秋涨，寂静地迅速流逝着。我的歌与我的爱情是一体，如溪流的潺湲，以他金色波涛的水流歌唱着。

——《爱者之贻》四 郑振铎 译

二〇〇九年六月，北京十月文艺出版社《新月集·飞鸟集》——

She is near to my heart as the meadow-flower to the earth; she is sweet to me as sleep is to tired limbs. My love for her is my life flowing in its fullness, like a river in autumn flood, running with serene abandonment. My songs are one with my love, like the murmur of a stream, that sings with all its waves and currents.

没有人永远活着，弟兄，没有东西能以经久。把这紧记在心及时行乐吧。

我们的生命不是那个旧的负担，我们的道路不是那条长的旅程。

一个单独的诗人，不必去唱一支旧歌。

花儿萎谢；但是戴花的人不必永远悲伤。

弟兄，把这个紧记在心及时行乐吧。

必须有一段完全的停歇，好把“圆满”编进音乐。

生命向它的黄昏下落，为了沉浸于金影之中。

必须从游戏中把“爱”召回，去饮忧伤之酒，再去生于泪天。

弟兄，把这紧记在心及时行乐吧。

我们忙去采花，怕被过路的风偷走。

去夺取稍纵即逝的接吻，使我们血液奔流双目发光。

我们的生命是热切的，愿望是强烈的，因为时间在敲着

离别之钟。

弟兄，把这紧记在心及时行乐吧。

我们没有时间去把握一件事物，揉碎它又把它丢在地上。

时间急速地走过。把梦幻藏在裙底。

我们的生命是短促的；只有几天恋爱的工夫。

若是为工作和劳役，生命就变得无尽的漫长。

弟兄，把这紧记在心及时行乐吧。

美对我们是甜柔的，因为她和我们生命的快速调子应节舞蹈。

知识对我们是宝贵的，因为我们永不会有时间去完成它。

一切都在永生的天上做完。但是大地的幻象的花朵，却被死亡保持得永远新鲜。

弟兄，把这紧记在心及时行乐吧。

——《园丁集》六八 冰心 译 一九五八年五月《泰戈尔诗选》——

None lives for ever, brother, and nothing lasts for long. Keep that in mind and rejoice.

Our life is not the one old burden, our path is not the one long journey.

One sole poet has not to sing one aged song.

The flower fades and dies; but he who wears the flower has not to mourn for it forever.

Brother, keep that in mind and rejoice.

There must come a full pause to weave perfection into music.

Life droops toward its sunset to be drowned in the golden shadows.

Love must be called from its play to drink sorrow and be borne to the heaven of tears.

Brother, keep that in mind and rejoice.

We hasten to gather our flowers lest they are plundered by the passing winds.

It quickens our blood and brightens our eyes to snatch kisses that would vanish if we delayed.

Our life is eager, our desires are keen, for time tolls the bell of parting.

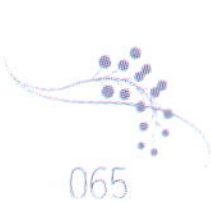

Brother, keep that in mind and rejoice.

There is not time for us to clasp a thing and crush it and fling it away to the dust.

The hours trip rapidly away, hiding their dreams in their skirts.

Our life is short; it yields but a few days for love.

Were it for work and drudgery it would be endlessly long.

Brother, keep that in mind and rejoice.

Beauty is sweet to us, because she dances to the same fleeting tune with our lives.

Knowledge is precious to us, because we shall never have time to complete it.

All is done and finished in the eternal Heaven. But earth's flowers of illusion are kept eternally fresh by death.

Brother, keep that in mind and rejoice.

我生命的生命，我要保持我的躯体永远纯洁，因为我知道你的生命的摩抚，接触着我的四肢。

我要永远从我的思想中屏除虚伪，因为我知道你就是那在我心中燃起理智之火的真理。

我要从我心中驱走一切的丑恶，使我的爱开花，因为我知道你在我的心宫深处安设了座位。

我要努力在我的行为上表现你，因为我知道是你的威力，给我力量来行动。

——《吉檀迦利》四 冰心 译 一九五五年四月——

Life of my life, I shall ever try to keep my body pure, knowing that thy living touch is upon all my limbs.

I shall ever try to keep all untruths out from my thoughts, knowing that thou art that truth which has kindled the light of reason in my mind.

I shall ever try to drive all evils away from my heart and keep my love in flower, knowing that thou hast thy seat in the inmost shrine of my heart.

And it shall be my endeavour to reveal thee in my actions, knowing it is thy power gives me strength to act.

若是你要忙着把水瓶灌满，来吧，到我的湖上来吧。

湖水将回绕在你的脚边，潺潺地说出它的秘密。

沙滩上有了欲来的雨云的阴影，云雾低垂在丛树的绿线上，像你眉上的浓发。

我深深地熟悉你脚步的韵律，它在我心中敲击。

来吧，到我的湖上来吧，如果你必须把水瓶灌满。

如果你想懒散闲坐，让你的水瓶漂浮在水面，来吧，到我的湖上来吧。

草坡碧绿，野花多得数不清。

你的思想将从你乌黑的眼眸中飞出，像鸟儿飞出窝巢。

你的披纱将褪落到脚上。

来吧，如果你要闲坐，到我的湖上来吧。

如果你想撇下嬉游跳进水里，来吧，到我的湖上来吧。

把你的蔚蓝的丝巾留在岸上；蔚蓝的水将没过你，盖住你。

水波将蹑足来吻你的颈项，在你耳边低语。

来吧，如果你想跳进水里，到我的湖上来吧。

如果你想发狂而投入死亡，来吧，到我的湖上来吧。

它是清凉的，深到无底。

它沉黑得像无梦的睡眠。

在它的深处黑夜就是白天，歌曲就是静默。

来吧，如果你想投入死亡，到我的湖上来吧。

——《园丁集》一二 冰心 译 一九五八年五月《泰戈尔诗选》——

If you would be busy and fill your pitcher, come, O come to my lake.

The water will cling round your feet and babble its secret.

The shadow of the coming rain is on the sands, and the clouds hang low upon the blue lines of the trees like the heavy hair above your eyebrows.

I know well the rhythm of your steps, they are beating in my heart.

Come, O come to my lake, if you must fill your pitcher.

If you would be idle and sit listless and let your pitcher float on the water, come, O come to my lake.

The grassy slope is green, and the wild flowers beyond number.

Your thoughts will stray out of your dark eyes like birds from their nests.

Your veil will drop to your feet.

Come, O come to my lake if you must sit idle.

If you would leave off your play and dive in the water, come, O come to my lake.

Let your blue mantle lie on the shore; the blue water

will cover you and hide you.

The waves will stand a-tiptoe to kiss your neck and whisper in your ears.

Come, O come to my lake, if you would dive in the water.

If you must be mad and leap to your death, come, O come to my lake.

It is cool and fathomlessly deep.

It is dark like a sleep that is dreamless.

There in its depths nights and days are one, and songs are silence.

Come, O come to my lake, if you would plunge to your death.

“你愿意把你的鲜花的花环挂在我的颈上么，佳人？”

“但是你要晓得，我编的那个花环，是为大家的，为那些偶然瞥见的人，住在未开发的大地上的人，住在诗人歌曲里的人。

现在来请求我的心作为答赠已经太晚了。

曾有一个时候我的生命像一朵蓓蕾，它所有的芬芳都储藏在花心里。

现在它已经远远地喷溢四散。

谁晓得有什么魅力，可以把它们收集关闭起来呢？

我的心不容我只给一个人，它是要给与许多人的。”

——《园丁集》三七 冰心 译 一九五八年五月《泰戈尔诗选》——

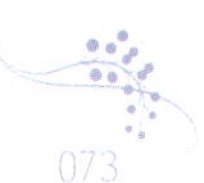

Would you put your wreath of fresh flowers on my neck, fair one?

But you must know that the one wreath that I had woven is for the many, for those who are seen in glimpses, or dwell in lands unexplored, or live in poets' songs.

It is too late to ask my heart in return for yours.

There was a time when my life was like a bud, all its perfume was stored in its core.

Now it is squandered far and wide.

Who knows the enchantment that can gather and shut it up again?

My heart is not mine to give to one only, it is given to the many.

我采了你的花，呵，世界！

我把它压在胸前，花刺伤了我。

日光渐暗，我发现花儿凋谢了，痛苦却存留着。

许多有香有色的花又将来到你这里，呵，世界。

但是我采花的时代过去了，黑夜悠悠，我没有了玫瑰，只有痛苦存留着。

——《园丁集》五七　冰心　译　一九五八五月《泰戈尔诗选》——

I plucked your flower, O world!

I pressed it to my heart and the thorn pricked.

When the day waned and it darkened, I found that the flower had faded, but the pain remained.

More flowers will come to you with perfume and pride, O world!

But my time for flower-gathering is over, and through the dark night I have not my rose, only the pain remains.

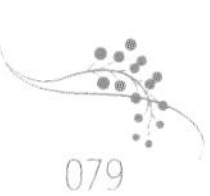



夜间黑漆漆的，你的微睡深沉在我身的安慰里。

醒吧，喂，爱情的痛苦，因为我不知道怎么样去开那扇门，我只好站在门外。

时间等着，群星守着，风静止着，沉默很沉重地压在我心里。

醒吧，爱情，醒吧！倒满我的空杯，用歌的呼吸激扰夜间吧。

——《采果集》二四 郑振铎 译

二〇〇九年六月，北京十月文艺出版社《新月集·飞鸟集》——

The night is dark and your slumber is deep in the bush of my being.

Wake, O Pain of Love, for I know not how to open the door, and I stand outside.

The hours wait, the stars watch, the wind is still, the silence is heavy in my heart.

Wake, Love, wake! Brim my empty cup, and with a breath of song ruffle the night.

安静吧，我的心，让别离的时间甜柔吧。

让它不是个死亡而是圆满。

让爱恋融入记忆，痛苦融入诗歌吧。

让穿越天空的飞翔在巢上敛翼中终止。

让你双手的最后的接触，像夜中花朵一样地温柔。

站住一会吧，呵，“美丽的结局”，用沉默说出最后的话语吧。

我向你鞠躬，举起我的灯来照亮你的归途。

——《园丁集》六一 冰心 译 一九五八年五月《泰戈尔诗选》——

Peace, my heart, let the time for the parting be sweet.

Let it not be a death but completeness.

Let love melt into memory and pain into songs.

Let the flight through the sky end in the folding of the wings over the nest.

Let the last touch of your hands be gentle like the flower of the night.

Stand still, O Beautiful End, for a moment, and say your last words in silence.

I bow to you and hold up my lamp to light you on your way.

早晨十点钟时，我沿着我们的街巷到学校里去，

每天在这个时候，我都遇见那个小贩，他叫道："镯子，透明的镯子！"

他不受事务的催促，他随意的走过这条街那条街，他没有一定的地方要去，他又没有一定的时间要回家。

我愿意我是一个小贩，在街上过日子，叫着，"镯子，透明的镯子！"

下午四点钟时，我从学校里

回家，

从一家门口，我看见一个园丁在那里掘地。

他用他的锄子，要怎么掘，便怎么掘，他被尘土污了衣裳，他或去晒太阳或是身上湿了，都没有人去骂他。

我愿意我是一个园丁，在花园里掘地，谁也不来阻止我。

天色刚黑时，母亲送我上床，

从开着的窗口，我能看见更夫在街上走来走去。

街上又黑又冷清，路灯立在那里，像一个头上生着一只红眼睛的巨人。

更夫摇着他的提灯，走来走去，他的影子也随在他身旁走着，他一生没有上床去过。

我愿意我是一个更夫，整夜在街上走，提了灯去追逐影子。

——《新月集·职业》郑振铎 译 一九二三年九月——

## VOCATION

When the gong sounds ten in the morning and I walk to school by our lane,

Everyday I meet the hawker crying, "Bangles, crystal bangles!"

There is nothing to hurry him on, there is no road he must take, no place he must go to, no time when he must come home.

I wish I were a hawker, spending my day in the road, crying, "Bangles, crystal bangles!"

When at four in the afternoon I come back from the school,

I can see through the gate of that house the gardener digging the ground.

He does what he likes with his spade, he soils his clothes with dust, nobody takes him to task if he gets baked in the sun or gets wet.

I wish I were a gardener digging away at the garden with nobody to stop me from digging.

Just as it gets dark in the evening and my mother sends

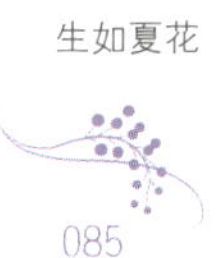



me to bed,

I can see through my open window the watchman walking up and down.

The lane is dark and lonely and the street-lamp stands like a giant with one red eye in its head.

The watchman swings his lantern and walks with his shadow at his side, and never once goes to bed in his life.

I wish I were a watchman walking the streets all night, chasing the shadows with my lantern.

在世界的谒见堂里，一根朴素的草叶，和阳光与夜半的星辰，坐在同一条毡褥上。

我的诗歌，也这样地和云彩与森林的音乐，在世界的心中平分席次。

但是，你这富有的人，你的财富，在太阳的喜悦的金光和沉思的月亮的柔光这种单纯的光彩里，却占不了一份。

包罗万象的天空的祝福，没有洒在它的上面。

等到死亡出现的时候，它就苍白枯萎，碎成尘土了。

——《园丁集》七四 冰心 译 一九五八年五月《泰戈尔诗选》——

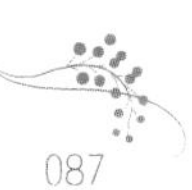



In the world's audience hall, the simple blade of grass sits on the same carpet with the sunbeam and the stars of midnight.

Thus my songs share their seats in the heart of the world with the music of the clouds and forests.

But, you man of riches, your wealth has no part in the simple grandeur of the sun's glad gold and the mellow gleam of the musing moon.

The blessing of all-embracing sky is not shed upon it.

And when death appears, it pales and withers and crumbles into dust.

你不过是一幅图画而不是如那些明星一样的真实，如这个灰尘一样的真实么？它们都随着万物的脉息而搏动着，但你则完全固定着你的静止的画成的形象。

你以前曾和我一同走着，你的呼吸温暖，你的肢体吟唱着生命之歌。我的世界，在你的语声里找到它的话语，用你的容光来接触我的心。你突然地停步不进了，伫立在永久的

荫旁，剩我一人向前走去。

生命如一个小孩，它笑着，一边跑着，一边喋喋地谈着死：它招呼我向前走去，我跟随着那不可见的脚步；但你立在那里，停在那些灰尘与明星之外，你不过是一幅图画。

不，那是不能够的。如果生命之流在你那里停止了，那么它便也要停止滚滚的河流，便也要停止具有色彩绚烂的足音的黎明的足迹了。如果你的头发的闪熠的微光在无望的黑暗中瞑灭了，那么夏天的绿荫也将和她的梦境一同死去了。

我忘了你，这会是真的么？我们匆匆地、头也不回地走着。忘了路旁篱落上开着的花。在忘掉一切的情景中，它们的香气不知不觉进入我们的呼吸，还充满着乐音。你已离开了我的世界，而去坐在我的生命的根上，所以这便是遗忘——回忆迷失在它自己的深处。

你已不再在我的歌声之前了，但你现在与他们是一个。你偕了晨光的第一条光线而到我这里来。到了夕阳的最后的金光消失时，我才不见了你。就是这时以后，我也仍在黑暗中寻求你。不，你不仅仅是一幅图画。

——《爱者之贻》四二 郑振铎 译

二〇〇九年六月，北京十月文艺出版社《新月集·飞鸟集》——

Are you a mere picture, and not as true as those stars, true as this dust? They throb with the pulse of things, but you are immensely aloof in your stillness, painted form.

The day was when you walked with me, your breath warm, your limbs singing of life. My world found its speech in your voice, and touched my heart with your face. You suddenly stopped in your walk, in the shadow-side of the Forever, and I went on alone.

Life,Like a child, laughs, shaking its rattle of death as it runs; it beckons me on , I follow the unseen; but you stand here, where you stopped behind that dust and those stars; and you are a mere picture.

No, it cannot be. Had the life-flood utterly stopped in you, it would stop the river in its flow, and the footfall of dawn in her cadence of colors. Had the glimmering dusk of your hair vanished in the hopeless dark, the woodland shade of summer would die with its dreams.

Can it be true that I forgot you? We haste on without heed, forgetting the flowers on the roadside hedge. Yet thy breathe unaware into our forgetfulness, filling it with music. You have moved from my world, to take seat at the root of my life, and therefore is this forgetting--remembrance lost in its own depth.

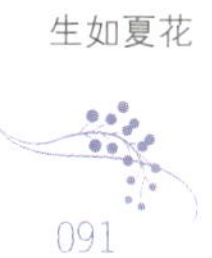



You are no longer before my songs, but one with them. You came to me with the first ray of dawn. I lost you with the last gold of evening. Ever since I am always finding you through the dark. No, you are no mere picture.

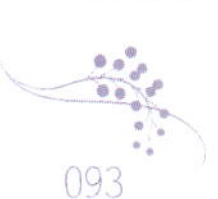

若是众人来晓得了我的王宫所在，那就要消灭在空气中去。

墙是白银做成的，屋顶是发光的金子。

王妃住在一座七重庭殿的宫中，她带的一颗宝石要值七个王国底财富。

但是，母亲，让我低声儿地把我王国底所在告诉给你。

那是在我们的土墩角上，杜茜花（TUlsi）盆放着的地方。

王女睡在七重通不过的海底远方的岸上。

除过我自己，世界中没有一个能发见她的。

她有镯子在她的腕儿上，真珠在她的耳朵儿里坠着；她的头发垂扫在地面上。

我用我的魔杖触她的时候，她便要醒来，她微笑的时候，宝石从她唇儿上坠落。

但是让我在你的耳朵儿边低声儿说罢，母亲；她是在那儿土墩角上杜茜花盆放着的地方。

你当往河边去行你的沐浴的时候到时，就请踏上屋顶的那个土墩儿。

我坐在墙影相交的角上。

只准小猫同我一道去，因为她知道仙话中的理发师住在什么地方。

但是让我低声儿，母亲，在你的耳朵里，说出仙话中的理发师住的地方。

那是在土墩儿角上杜茜盆放着的地方。

——《新月集·仙境》郑振铎 译 一九二二年二月——

FAIRYLAND

If people came to know where my king's palace is, it would vanish into the air.

The walls are of white silver and the roof of shining gold.

The queen lives in a palace with seven courtyards, and she wears a jewel that cost all the wealth of seven kingdoms.

But, let me tell you, mother, in a whisper, where my king's palace is.

It is at the corner of our terrace where the pot of the

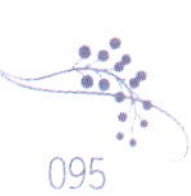



tulsi plant stands.

The princess lies sleeping on the faraway shore of the seven impassable seas.

There is none in the world who can find her but myself.

She has bracelets on her arms and pearl drops in her ears; her hair sweeps down upon the floor.

She will wake when I touch her with my magic wand, and jewels will fall from her lips when she smiles.

But let me whisper in your ear, mother; she is there in the corner of our terrace where the pot of the tulsi plant stands.

When it is time for you to go to the river for your bath, step up to that terrace on the roof.

I sit on the corner where the shadows of the walls meet together.

Only puss is allowed to come with me, for she knows where the barber in the story lives.

But let me whisper, mother, in your ear where the barber in the story lives.

It is at the corner of the terrace where the pot of the tulsi plant stands.

真与幻·爱情

早晨我把网撒在海里。

我从沉黑的深渊拉出奇形奇美的东西——有些微笑般地发亮，有些眼泪般地闪光，有的晕红得像新娘的双颊。

当我携带着这一天的担负回到家里的时候，我爱正坐在园里悠闲地扯着花叶。

我沉吟了一会，就把我捞得的一切放在她的脚前，沉默地站着。

她瞥了一眼说，“这是些什么怪东西？我不知道这些东西有什么用处！”

我羞愧得低了头，心想，“我并没有为这些东西去奋斗，也不是从市场里买来的；这不是一些配送给她的礼物。”

整夜的工夫我把这些东西一件一件地丢到街上。

早晨行路的人来了；他们把这些拾起带到远方去了。

——《园丁集》三 冰心 译 一九五八年五月《泰戈尔诗选》——

In the morning I cast my net into the sea.

I dragged up from the dark abyss things of strange aspect and strange beauty–some shone like a smile, some glistened like tears, and some were flushed like the cheeks of a bride.

When with the day's burden I went home, my love was sitting in the garden idly tearing the leaves of a flower.

I hesitated for a moment, and then placed at her feet all that I had dragged up, and stood silent.

She glanced at them and said, "What strange things are these? I know not of what use they are!"

I bowed my head in shame and thought, "I have not fought for these, I did not buy them in the market; they are not fit gifts for her."

Then the whole night through I flung them one by one into the street.

In the morning travellers came; they picked them up and carried them into far countries.

威权对世界说道，“你是我的。”

世界把威权囚禁在座位之下。

爱情对世界说道，“我是你的。”

世界却给爱情以她屋内的自由。

——《飞鸟集》九三 郑振铎 译 一九二二年六月——

Power said to the world, “Your are mine.” The world kept it prisoner on her throne. Love said to the world, “I am thine.” The world gave it the freedom of her house.

手握着手，眼恋着眼：这样开始了我们的心的纪录。

这是三月的月明之夜；空气时有凤仙花的芬芳；我的横笛抛在地上，你的花串也没有编成。

你我之间的爱像歌曲一样地单纯。

你橙黄色的面纱使我眼睛陶醉。

你给我编的茉莉花环使我心震颤，像是受了赞扬。

这是一个又予又留，又隐又现的游戏；有些微笑，有些娇羞，也有些甜柔的无用的抵拦。

你我之间的爱像歌曲一样地单纯。

没有现在以外的神秘；不强求那做不到的事情；没有魅惑后面的阴影；没有黑暗深处的探索。

你我之间的爱像歌曲一样地单纯。

我们没有走出一切语言之外进入永远的沉默；我们没有

向空举手寻求希望以外的东西。

我们付与，我们取得，这就够了。

我们没有把喜乐压成微尘来榨取痛苦之酒。

你我之间的爱像歌曲一样地单纯。

——《园丁集》一六 冰心 译 一九五八年五月《泰戈尔诗选》——

Hands cling to hands and eyes linger on eyes: thus begins the record of our hearts.

It is the moonlit night of March; the sweet smell of henna is in the air; my flute lies on the earth neglected and your garland of flowers is unfinished.

This love between you and me is simple as a song.

Your veil of the saffron colour makes my eyes drunk.

The jasmine wreath that you wove me thrills to my heart like praise.

It is a game of giving and withholding, revealing and screening again; some smiles and some little shyness, and some sweet useless struggles.

This love between you and me is simple as a song.

No mystery beyond the present; no striving for the

impossible; no shadow behind the charm; no groping in the depth of the dark.

This love between you and me is simple as a song.

We do not stray out of all words into the ever silent; we do not raise our hands to the void for things beyond hope.

It is enough what we give and we get.

We have not crushed the joy to the utmost to wring from it the wine of pain.

This love between you and me is simple as a song.

呵，这些茉莉花，这些白的茉莉花！

我似乎忆起我第一次双手满捧着这些茉莉花，这些白的茉莉花的时候。

我喜爱那日光，那天空，那绿色的大地；

我听见那河水淙净的流声，在黑漆的中夜里传过来；

我看见那秋天的夕阳，在荒野的路角，映照在我的身上，如新妇揭起她的面网迎接她的爱人。

但我想起孩提时第一次捧在手里的白茉莉，心里还感着甜蜜的回忆。

我生平有过许多快活的日子，在宴会的晚上，我跟了说笑话的人而大笑。

在灰暗的雨晨，我吟哦着许多飘逸的诗篇。

我颈上戴过爱人手织的夜晚的醉花[1]的花圈，

但我想起孩提时第一次捧在手里的白茉莉，心里还感着甜蜜的回忆。

——《新月集·第一次的茉莉》郑振铎 译 一九二三年九月——

①醉花（bakula），学名mimusopselengi。印度传说美女口中吐出香液，此花始开。

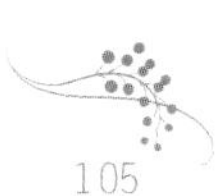

## THE FIRST JASMINES

Ah, these jasmines, these white jasmines!

I seem to remember the first day when I filled my hands with these jasmines, these white jasmines.

I have loved the sunlight, the sky and the green earth;

I have heard the liquid murmur of the river through the darkness of midnight;

Autumn sunsets have come to me at the bend of a road in the lonely waste, like a bride raising her veil to accept her lover.

Yet my memory is still sweet with the first white jasmines that I held in my hand when I was a child.

Many a glad day has come in my life, and I have laughed with merrymakers on festival nights.

On grey mornings of rain I have crooned many an idle song.

I have worn round my neck the evening wreath of bakulas woven by the hand of love.

Yet my heart is sweet with the memory of the first fresh jasmines that filled my hands when I was a child.

不要不辞而别，我爱。

我看望了一夜，现在我眼上睡意重重。

只恐我在睡中把你丢失了。

不要不辞而别，我爱。

我惊起伸出双手去摸触你，我问自己说，“这是一个梦么？”

但愿我能用我的心系住你的双足，紧抱在胸前！

不要不辞而别，我爱。

——《园丁集》三四 冰心 译 一九五八年五月《泰戈尔诗选》——

Do not go, my love, without asking my leave.

I have watched all night, and now my eyes are heavy with sleep.

I fear lest I lose you when I am sleeping.

Do not go, my love, without asking my leave.

I start up and stretch my hands to touch you. I ask myself, "Is it a dream?"

Could I but entangle your feet with my heart and hold them fast to my breast!

Do not go, my love, without asking my leave.

春花开放出来，如不言之爱的热烈的苦痛。我旧时歌声的回忆，随了他们的呼吸而俱来。我的心突然长出欲望的绿叶来。我的爱没有来，但她的接触是在我的肢体上，她的语声也横过芬芳的田野而到来。她的眼波在天空的忧愁的深处；但是她的眼睛在哪里呢？她的吻香飞熠在空气之中，但是她的樱唇在哪里呢？

——《爱者之贻》三十 郑振铎 译

二〇〇九年六月，北京十月文艺出版社《新月集·飞鸟集》——

The spring flowers break out like the passionate pain of unspoken love. With their breath comes the memory of my old day songs. My hearts of a sudden has put on green leaves of the sky, but where are her eyes? Her kisses flit in the air, but where are her lips?

“即使爱只给你带来了哀愁，也信任它。不要把你的心关起。”

“呵，不，我的朋友，你的话语太隐晦了，我不懂得。”

“心是应该和一滴眼泪，一首诗歌一起送给人的，我爱。”

“呵，不，我的朋友，你的话语太隐晦了，我不懂得。”

“喜乐像露珠一样地脆弱，它在欢笑中死去。哀愁却是坚强而耐久。让含愁的爱在你眼中醒起吧。”

“呵，不，我的朋友，你的话语太隐晦了，我不懂得。”

“荷花在日中开放，丢掉了自己的一切所有。在永生的冬雾里，它将不再含苞。”

“呵，不，我的朋友，你的话语太隐晦了，我不懂得。”

——《园丁集》二七　冰心　译　一九五八年五月《泰戈尔诗选》——

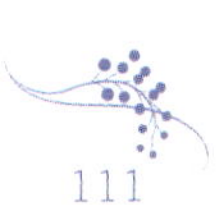

"Trust love even if it brings sorrow. Do not close up your heart."

"Ah, no, my friend, your words are dark, I cannot understand them."

"The heart is only for giving away with a tear and a song, my love."

"Ah, no, my friend, your words are dark, I cannot understand them."

"Pleasure is frail like a dewdrop, while it laughs it dies. But sorrow is strong and abiding. Let sorrowful love wake in your eyes."

"Ah, no, my friend, your words are dark, I cannot understand them."

"The lotus blooms in the sight of the sun, and loses all that it has. It would not remain in bud in the eternal winter mist."

"Ah, no, my friend, your words are dark, I cannot understand them."

云霾堆积，黑暗渐深。呵，爱，你为什么让我独在门外等候?

在中午工作最忙的时候，我和大家在一起，但在这黑暗寂寞的日子，我只企望着你。

若是你不容我见面，若是你完全把我抛弃，我真不知将如何度过这悠长的雨天。

我不住地凝望遥远的阴空，我的心和不宁的风一同彷徨悲叹。

——《吉檀迦利》一八 冰心 译 一九五五年四月——

Clouds heap upon clouds and it darkens. Ah, love, why dost thou let me wait outside at the door all alone?

In the busy moments of the noontide work I am with the crowd, but on this dark lonely day it is only for thee that I hope.

If thou showest me not thy face, if thou leavest me wholly aside, I know not how I am to pass these long, rainy hours.

I keep gazing on the faraway gloom of the sky, and my heart wanders wailing with the restless wind.

爱情呀！当你手里拿着点亮了的痛苦之灯走来时，我能够看见你的脸，而且以你为快乐的。

——《飞鸟集》一六二 郑振铎 译 一九二二年六月 ——

Love! When you come with the burning lamp of pain in your hand, I can see your face and know you as bliss.

灯火，灯火在哪里呢？用熊熊的渴望之火把它点上罢！

灯在这里，却没有一丝火焰，——这是你的命运吗，我的心呵！你还不如死了好！

悲哀在你门上敲着，她传话说你的主醒着呢，他叫你在夜的黑暗中奔赴爱的约会。

云雾遮满天空，雨也不停的下。我不知道我心里有什么在动荡，——我不懂得它的意义。

一霎的电光，在我的视线上抛下一道更深的黑暗，我的心摸索着寻找那夜的音乐对我呼唤的径路。

灯火，灯火在哪里呢？用熊熊的渴望之火把它点上罢！雷声在响，狂风怒吼着穿过天空。夜像黑岩一般的黑。不要让时间在黑暗中度过罢。用你的生命把爱的灯点上罢。

——《吉檀迦利》二七 冰心 译 一九五五年四月 ——

Light, oh where is the light? Kindle it with the burning fire of desire!

There is the lamp but never a flicker of a flame–is such thy fate, my heart! Ah, death were better by far for thee!

Misery knocks at thy door, and her message is that thy lord is wakeful, and he calls thee to thy love-tryst through the darkness of night.

The sky is overcast with clouds and the rain is ceaseless. I know not what this is that stirs in me–I know not its meaning.

A moment's flash of lightning drags down a deeper gloom on my sight, and my heart gropes for the path to where the music of the night calls me.

Light, oh where is the light! Kindle it with the burning fire of desire! It thunders and the wind rushes screaming through the void. The night is black as a  black stone. Let not the hours pass by in the dark. Kindle the lamp of love with thy life.

我爱你，我的爱人。请饶恕我的爱。

像一只迷路的鸟，我被捉住了。

当我的心抖战的时候，它丢了围纱，变成赤裸。用怜悯遮住它吧。爱人，请饶恕我的爱。

如果你不能爱我，爱人，请饶恕我的痛苦。

不要远远地斜视我。

我将偷偷地回到我的角落里去，在黑暗中坐地。

我将用双手掩起我赤裸的羞惭。

回过脸去吧，我的爱人，请饶恕我的痛苦。

如果你爱我，爱人，请饶恕我的欢乐。

当我的心被快乐的洪水卷走的时候，不要笑我的汹涌的退却。

当我坐在宝座上，用我暴虐的爱来统治你的时候，当我像女神一样向你施恩的时候，饶恕我的骄傲吧，爱人，也饶恕我的快乐。

——《园丁集》三三　冰心 译　一九五八年五月《泰戈尔诗选》——

I love you, beloved. Forgive me my love.

Like a bird losing its way I am caught.

When my heart was shaken it lost its veil and was naked. Cover it with pity, beloved, and forgive me my love.

If you cannot love me, beloved, forgive me my pain.

Do not look askance at me from afar.

I will steal back to my corner and sit in the dark.

With both hands I will cover my naked shame.

Turn your face from me, beloved, and forgive me my pain.

If you love me, beloved, forgive me my joy.

When my heart is borne away by the flood of happiness, do not smile at my perilous abandonment.

When I sit on my throne and rule you with my tyranny of love, when like a goddess I grant you my favour, bear with my pride, beloved, and forgive me my joy.

驯养的鸟在笼里，自由的鸟在林中。

时间到了，他们相会，这是命中注定的。

自由的鸟说，“呵，我爱，让我们飞到林中去吧。”

笼中的鸟低声说，“到这里来吧，让我俩都住在笼里。”

自由的鸟说，“在栅栏中间，哪有展翅的余地呢？”

“可怜呵，”笼中的鸟说，“在天空中我不晓得到哪里去栖息。”

自由的鸟叫唤说，“我的宝贝，唱起林野之歌吧。”

笼中的鸟说，“坐在我旁边吧，我要教你说学者的语言。”

自由的鸟叫唤说，“不，不！歌曲是不能传授的。”

笼中的鸟说，“可怜的我呵，我不会唱林野

之歌。"

他们的爱情因渴望而更加热烈，但是他们永不能比翼双飞。

他们隔栏相望，而他们相知的愿望是虚空的。

他们在依恋中振翼，唱说，"靠近些吧，我爱！"

自由的鸟叫唤说，"这是做不到的，我怕这笼子的紧闭的门。"

笼里的鸟低声说，"我的翅翼是无力的，而且已经死去了。"

——《园丁集》六 冰心 译 一九五八年五月《泰戈尔诗选》——

The tame bird was in a cage, the free bird was in the forest.

They met when the time came, it was a decree of fate.

The free bird cries, "O my love, let us fly to wood."

The cage bird whispers, "Come hither, let us both live in the cage."

Says the free bird, "Among bars, where is there room to spread one's wings?"

"Alas," cries the cage bird, "I should not know where to sit perched in the sky."

The free bird cries, "My darling, sing the songs of the woodlands."

The cage bird says, "Sit by my side. I'll teach you the speech of the learned."

The forest bird cries, "No, ah no! Songs can never be taught."

The cage bird says, "Alas for me, I know not the songs of the woodlands."

Their love is intense with longing, but they never can fly wing to wing.

Through the bars of the cage they look, and vain is their wish to know each other.

They flutter their wings in yearning, and sing, "Come closer, my love!"

The free bird cries, "It cannot be, I fear the closed doors of the cage."

The cage bird whispers, "Alas, my wings are powerless and dead."

他天天来了又走了。

去吧，把我头上的花朵送去给他吧，我的朋友。

假如他问赠花的人是谁，我请你不要把我的名字告诉他——因为他来了又要走的。

他坐在树下的地上。

用繁花密叶给他敷设一个座位吧，我的朋友。

他的眼神是忧郁的，它把忧郁带到我的心中。

他没有说出他的心事；他只是来了又走了。

——《园丁集》二〇 冰心 译 一九五八年五月《泰戈尔诗选》——

Day after day he comes and goes away.

Go, and give him a flower from my hair, my friend.

If he asks who was it that sent it, I entreat you do not tell him my name—for he only comes and goes away.

He sits on the dust under the tree.

Spread there a seat with flowers and leaves, my friend.

His eyes are sad, and they bring sadness to my heart.

He does not speak what he has in mind; he only comes and goes away.

他为什么特地来到我的门前，这年轻的游子，当天色黎明的时候？

每次我进出经过他的身旁，我的眼睛总被他的面庞所吸引。

我不知道我是应该同他说话还是保持沉默。他为什么特地到我门前来呢？

七月的阴夜是黑沉的；秋日的天空是浅蓝的；南风把春天吹得骀荡不宁。

他每次用新调编着新歌。

我放下活计眼里充满雾水。他为什么特地到我门前来呢？

——《园丁集》二一 冰心译 一九五八年五月《泰戈尔诗选》——

Why did he choose to come to my door, the wandering youth, when the day dawned?

As I come in and out I pass by him every time, and my eyes are caught by his face.

I know not if I should speak to him or keep silent. Why did he choose to come to my door?

The cloudy nights in July are dark; the sky is soft blue in the autumn; the spring days are restless with the south wind.

He weaves his songs with fresh tunes every time.

I turn from my work and my eyes fill with the mist. Why did he choose to come to my door?

当她用急步走过我的身旁，她的裙缘触到了我。

从一颗心的无名小岛上忽然吹来一阵春天的温馨。

一霎飞触的撩乱扫拂过我，立刻又消失了，像扯落的花瓣在和风中飘扬。

它落在我的心上，像她的身躯的叹息和她的心灵的低语。

——《园丁集》二二 冰心译 一九五八年五月《泰戈尔诗选》——

When she passed by me with quick steps, the end of her skirt touched me.

From the unknown island of a heart came a sudden warm breath of spring.

A flutter of a flitting touch brushed me and vanished in a moment, like a torn flower petal blown in the breeze.

It fell upon my heart like a sigh of her body and whisper of her heart.

你为什么悠闲地坐在那里，把镯子玩得叮当作响呢？

把你的水瓶灌满了吧。是你应当回家的时候了。

你为什么悠闲地拨弄着水玩，偷偷地瞀视路上的行人呢？

灌满你的水瓶回家去吧。

早晨的时间过去了——沉黑的水不住地流逝。

波浪相互低语嬉笑闲玩着。

流荡的云片聚集在远野高地的天边。

它们留连着悠闲地看着你的脸微笑着。

灌满你的水瓶回家去吧。

——《园丁集》二三 冰心 译 一九五八年五月《泰戈尔诗选》——

Why do you sit there and jingle your bracelets in mere idle sport?

Fill your pitcher. It is time for you to come home.

Why do you stir the water with your hands and fitfully glance at the road for some one in mere idle sport?

Fill your pitcher and come home.

The morning hours pass by—the dark water flows on.

The waves are laughing and whispering to each other in mere idle sport.

The wandering clouds have gathered at the edge of the sky on yonder rise of the land.

They linger and look at your face and smile in mere idle sport.

Fill your pitcher and come home.

不要把你心的秘密藏起，我的朋友！

对我说吧，秘密地对我一个人说吧。

你这个笑得这样温柔，说得这样轻软的人，我的心将听着你的言语，不是我的耳朵。

夜深沉，庭宁静，鸟巢也被睡眠笼罩着。

从踌躇的眼泪里，从沉吟的微笑里，从甜柔的羞怯和痛苦里，把你心的秘密告诉我吧！

——《园丁集》二四 冰心译 一九五八年五月《泰戈尔诗选》——

Do not keep to yourself the secret of your heart, my friend!

Say it to me, only to me, in secret.

You who smile so gently, softly whisper, my heart will hear it, not my ears.

The night is deep, the house is silent, the birds' nests are shrouded with sleep.

Speak to me through hesitating tears, through faltering smiles, through sweet shame and pain, the secret of your heart!

你的疑问的眼光是含愁的。它要追探了解我的意思，好像月亮探测大海。

我已经把我生命的终始，全部暴露在你的眼前，没有任何隐秘和保留。因此你不认识我。

假如它是一块宝石，我就能把它碎成千百颗粒，穿成项链挂在你的颈上。

假如它是一朵花，圆圆小小香香的，我就能从枝上采来戴在你的发上。

但是它是一颗心，我的爱人。何处是它的边和底?

你不知道这个王国的边极，但你仍是这王国的女王。

假如它是片刻的欢娱，它将在喜笑中开花，你立刻就会看到、懂得了。

假如它是一阵痛苦，它将融化成晶莹的眼泪，不着一字地反映出它最深的秘密。

但是它是爱，我的爱人。

它的欢乐和痛苦是无边的，它的需求和财富是无尽的。

它和你亲近得像你的生命一样，但是你永远不能完全了解它。

——《园丁集》二八 冰心 译 一九五八年五月《泰戈尔诗选》——

Your questioning eyes are sad. They seek to know my meaning as the moon would fathom the sea.

I have bared my life before your eyes from end to end, with nothing hidden or held back. That is why you know me not.

If it were only a gem, I could break it into a hundred pieces and string them into a chain to put on your neck.

If it were only a flower, round and small and sweet, I could pluck it from its stem to set it in your hair.

But it is a heart, my beloved. Where are its shores and its bottom?

You know not the limits of this kingdom, still you are its queen.

If it were only a moment of pleasure it would flower in an easy smile, and you could see it and read it in a moment.

If it were merely a pain it would melt in limpid tears, reflecting its inmost secret without a word.

But it is love, my beloved.

Its pleasure and pain are boundless, and endless its wants and wealth.

It is as near to you as your life, but you can never wholly know it.

只恐我太容易地认得你，你对我耍花招。

你用欢笑的闪光使我目盲来掩盖你的眼泪。

我知道，我知道你的妙计，

你从来不说出你所要说的话。

只恐我不珍爱你，你千方百计地闪避我。

只恐我把你和大家混在一起，你独自站在一边。

我知道，我知道你的妙计，

你从来不走你所要走的路。

你的要求比别人都多，因此你才静默。

你用嬉笑的无心来回避我的赠与。

我知道，我知道你的妙计，

你从来不肯接受你想接受的东西。

——《园丁集》三五 冰心 译 一九五八年五月《泰戈尔诗选》——

Lest I should know you too easily, you play with me.
You blind me with flashes of laughter to hide your tears.
I know, I know your art,
You never say the word you would.

Lest I should not prize you, you elude me in a thousand ways.
Lest I should confuse you with the crowd, you stand aside.
I know, I know your art,
You never walk the path you would.

Your claim is more than that of others, that is why you are silent.
With playful carelessness you avoid my gifts.
I know, I know your art,
You never will take what you would.

“我相信你的爱，”让这句话做我的最后的话。

——《飞鸟集》三二六 郑振铎 译 一九二二年六月——

Let this be my last word, that I trust in thy love.

# 短而长·旅途

行路人，你必须走么?

夜是静寂的，黑暗在树林上昏睡。

我们的凉台上灯火辉煌，繁花鲜美，青春的眼睛还清醒着。

你离开的时间到了么?

行路人，你必须走么?

我们不曾用恳求的手臂来抱住你的双足。

你的门开着。你的立在门外的马，也已上了鞍鞯。

如果我们想拦住你的去路，也只是用我们的歌曲。

如果我们曾想挽留你，也只是用我们的眼睛。

行路人，我们没有希望留住你，我们只有眼泪。

在你眼里发光的是什么样的不灭之火?

在你血管中奔流的是什么样的不宁的热力?

从黑暗中有什么召唤在引动你?

你从天上的星星中，念到什么可怕的咒语，就是黑夜沉默而异样地走进你心中时带来的那个密封的秘密的消息?

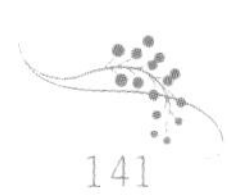



如果你不喜欢那热闹的集会，如果你需要安静，困乏的心呵，我们就吹灭灯火，停止琴声。

我们将在风叶声中静坐在黑暗里，倦乏的月亮将在你窗上洒上苍白的光辉。

呵，行路人，是什么不眠的精灵从中夜的心中和你接触了呢?

——《园丁集》六三 冰心 译 一九五八年五月《泰戈尔诗选》——

Traveller, must you go?

The night is still and the darkness swoons upon the forest.

The lamps are bright in our balcony, the flowers all fresh, and the youthful eyes still awake.

Is the time for your parting come?

Traveller, must you go?

We have not bound your feet with our entreating arms.

Your doors are open. Your horse stands saddled at the gate.

If we have tried to bar your passage, it was but with our songs.

Did we ever try to hold you back, it was but with our eyes.

Traveller, we are helpless to keep you. We have only

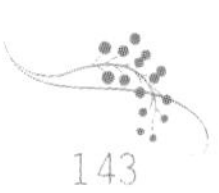



our tears.

What quenchless fire glows in your eyes?

What restless fever runs in your blood?

What call from the dark urges you?

What awful incantation have you read among the stars in the sky, that with a sealed secret message the night entered your heart, silent and strange?

If you do not care for merry meetings, if you must have peace, weary heart, we shall put our lamps out and silence our harps.

We shall sit still in the dark in the rustle of leaves, and the tired moon will shed pale rays on your window.

O traveller, what sleepless spirit has touched you from the heart of the midnight?

您曾经带领着我，穿过我的白天的拥挤不堪的旅行，而到达了我的黄昏的孤寂之境。

在通宵的寂静里，我等待着它的意义。

——《飞鸟集》二四一 郑振铎 译 一九五六年七月——

Thou hast led me through my crowded travels of the day to my evening's loneliness. I wait for its meaning through the stillness of the night.

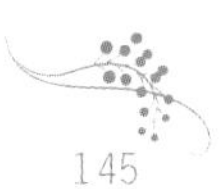



这是你的脚凳，你在最贫最贱最失所的人群中歇足。

我想向你鞠躬，我的敬礼不能达到你歇足地方的深处——那最贫最贱最失所的人群中。

你穿着破敝的衣服，在最贫最贱最失所的人群中行走，骄傲永远不能走近这个地方。

你和那最没有朋友的最贫最贱最失所的人们作伴，我的心永远找不到那个地方。

——《吉檀迦利》一〇 冰心 译 一九五五年四月——

Here is thy footstool and there rest thy feet where live the poorest, and lowliest, and lost.

When I try to bow to thee, my obeisance cannot reach down to the depth where thy feet rest among the poorest, and lowliest, and lost.

Pride can never approach to where thou walkest in the clothes of the humble among the poorest, and lowliest, and lost.

My heart can never find its way to where thou keepest company with the companionless among the poorest, the lowliest, and the lost.

我心绪不宁。我渴望着遥远的事物。

我的灵魂在极想中走出，要去摸触幽暗的远处的边缘。

呵，“伟大的来生”，呵，你笛声的高亢的呼唤！

我忘却了，我总是忘却了，我没有奋飞的翅翼，我永远在这地点系住。

我切望而又清醒，我是一个异乡的异客。

你的气息向我低语出一个不可能的希望。

我的心懂得你的语言就像它懂得自己的语言一样。

呵，“遥远的寻求”，呵，你笛声的高亢的呼唤！

我忘却了，我总是忘却了，我不认得路，我也没有生翼的马。

我心绪不宁。我是自己心中的流浪者。

在疲倦时光的日霭中，你广大的幻象在天空的蔚蓝中显现！

呵，“最远的尽头”，呵，你笛声的高亢的呼唤！

我忘却了，我总是忘却了，在我独居的房子里，所有的门户都是紧闭的！

——《园丁集》五 冰心 译 一九五八年五月《泰戈尔诗选》——

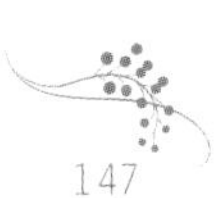

I am restless. I am athirst for faraway things.

My soul goes out in a longing to touch the skirt of the dim distance.

O Great Beyond. O the keen call of thy flute!

I forget, I ever forget, that I have no wings to fly, that I am bound in this spot evermore.

I am eager and wakeful. I am a stranger in a strange land.

Thy breath comes to me whispering an impossible hope.

Thy tongue is known to my heart as its very own.

O Far-to-seek, O the keen call of thy flute!

I forget, I ever forget, that I know not the way, that I have not the winged horse.

I am listless, I am a wanderer in my heart.

In the sunny haze of the languid hours, what vast vision of thine takes shape in the blue of the sky!

O Farthest End, O the keen call of thy flute!

I forget, I ever forget, that the gates are shut everywhere in the house where I dwell alone!

我的昼间之花，垂下他的花瓣，忘了一切。

在黄昏中，这花成熟为记忆金色的果实。

——《飞鸟集》一八一 郑振铎 译 一九二二年六月 ——

My flower of the day dropped its petals forgotten. In the evening it ripens into a golden fruit of memory.

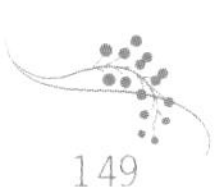



在这暴风雨的夜晚你还在外面作爱的旅行吗，我的朋友？天空像失望者在哀号。

我今夜无眠。我不断的开门向黑暗中瞭望，我的朋友！

我什么都看不见。我不知道你要走哪一条路！

是从墨黑的河岸上，是从远远的愁惨的树林边，是穿过昏暗迂回的曲径，你摸索着来到我这里吗，我的朋友？

——《吉檀迦利》二三 冰心 译 一九五五年四月——

Art thou abroad on this stormy night on the journey of love, my friend? The sky groans like one in despair.

I have no sleep tonight. Ever and again I open my door and look out on the darkness, my friend!

I can see nothing before me. I wonder where lies thy path!

By what dim shore of the ink-black river, by what far edge of the frowning forest, through what mazy depth of gloom art thou threading thy course to come to me, my friend?

不，我的朋友，我永不会做一个苦行者，随便你怎么说。

我将永不做一个苦行者，假如她不和我一同受戒。

这是我坚定的决心，如果我找不到一个阴凉的住处和一个忏悔的伴侣，我将永不会变成一个苦行者。

不，我的朋友，我将永不离开我的炉火与家庭，去退隐到深林里面，如果在林荫中没有欢笑的回响；如果没有郁金色的衣裙在风中飘扬；如果它的幽静不因有轻柔的微语而加深。

我将永不会做一个苦行者。

——《园丁集》四三　冰心　译　一九五八年五月《泰戈尔诗选》——

No, my friends, I shall never be an ascetic, whatever you may say.

I shall never be an ascetic if she does not take the vow with me.

It is my firm resolve that if I cannot find a shady shelter and a companion for my penance, I shall never turn ascetic.

No, my friends, I shall never leave my hearth and home, and retire into the forest solitude, if rings no merry laughter in its echoing shade and if the end of no saffron mantle flutters in the wind; if its silence is not deepened by soft whispers.

I shall never be an ascetic.

为什么盯着我使我羞愧呢？
我不是来求乞的。
只为要消磨时光，我才来站在你院边的篱外。
为什么盯着我使我羞愧呢？

我没有从你园里采走一朵玫瑰，没有摘下一颗果子。
我谦卑地在任何生客都可站立的路边棚下，找个荫蔽。
我没有采走一朵玫瑰。

是的，我的脚疲乏了，骤雨又落了下来。
风在摇曳的竹林中呼叫。
云阵像败退似的跑过天空。
我的脚疲乏了。

我不知道你怎样看待我，或是你在门口等什么人。
闪电昏眩了你看望的目光。
我怎能知道你会看到站在黑暗中的我呢？
我不知道你怎样看待我。

白日过尽，雨势暂停。

我离开你园畔的树荫和草地上的座位。

日光已暗；关上你的门户吧；我走我的路。

白日过尽了。

——《园丁集》五三 冰心 译 一九五八五月《泰戈尔诗选》——

Why do you put me to shame with a look?

I have not come as a beggar.

Only for a passing hour I stood at the end of your courtyard outside the garden hedge.

Why do you put me to shame with a look?

Not a rose did I gather from your garden, not a fruit did I pluck.

I humbly took my shelter under the wayside shade where every strange traveller may stand.

Not a rose did I pluck.

Yes, my feet were tired, and the shower of rain came down.

The winds cried out among the swaying bamboo branches.

The clouds ran across the sky as though in the flight from defeat.

My feet were tired.

I know not what you thought of me or for whom you were waiting at your door.

Flashes of lightning dazzled your watching eyes.

How could I know that you could see me where I stood in the dark?

I know not what you thought of me.

The day is ended, and the rain has ceased for a moment.

I leave the shadow of the tree at the end of your garden and this seat on the grass.

It has darkened; shut your door; I go my way.

The day is ended.

在这个黄昏的朦胧里，好些东西看来都有些幻相——尖塔的底层在黑暗里消失了，树顶像墨水的斑点似的。我将等待着黎明，而当我醒来的时候，就会看到在光明里的您的城市。

——《飞鸟集》三二一 郑振铎 译 一九五六年七月——

Things look phantastic in this dimness of the dusk–the spires whose bases are lost in the dark and treetops like blots of ink. I shall wait for the morning and wake up to see thy city in the light.

我真烦，为什么他们把我的房子盖在通向市镇的路边呢?

他们把满载的船只拴在我的树上。

他们任意地来去游逛。

我坐着看着他们；光阴都消磨了。

我不能回绝他们。这样我的日子便过去了。

日日夜夜他们的足音在我门前震荡。

我徒然地叫道，“我不认得你们。”

有些人是我的手指所认识的，有些人是我的鼻官所认识的，我脉管中的血液似乎认得他们，有些人是我的魂梦所认识的。

我不能回绝他们。我呼唤他们说，“谁愿意到我房子里来就请来吧，对了，来吧。”

清晨庙里的钟声敲起。

他们提着筐子来了。

他们的脚像玫瑰般红。熹微的晨光照在他们的脸上。

我不能回绝他们。我呼唤他们说，“到我园里来采花吧。到这里来吧。”

中午锣声在庙殿门前敲起。

我不知道他们为什么放下工作在我篱畔留连。

他们发上的花朵已经褪色枯萎了；他们横笛里的音调也显得乏倦。

我不能回绝他们。我呼唤他们说，“我的树荫下是凉爽的。来吧，朋友们。”

夜里蟋蟀在林中唧唧地叫。

是谁慢慢地来到我的门前轻轻地敲叩？

我模糊地看到他的脸，他一句话也没说，四周是天空的静默。

我不能回绝我的沉默的客人。我从黑暗中望着他的脸，梦幻的时间过去了。

——《园丁集》四 冰心 译 一九五八年五月《泰戈尔诗选》——

Ah me, why did they build my house by the road to the market town?

They moor their laden boats near my trees.

They come and go and wander at their will.

I sit and watch them; my time wears on.

Turn them away I cannot. And thus my days pass by.

Night and day their steps sound by my door.

Vainly I cry, "I do not know you."

Some of them are known to my fingers, some to my nostrils, the blood in my veins seems to know them, and some are known to my dreams.

Turn them away I cannot. I call them and say, "Come to my house whoever chooses. Yes, come."

In the morning the bell rings in the temple.

They come with their baskets in their hands.

Their feet are rosy-red. The early light of dawn is on their faces.

Turn them away I cannot. I call them and I say, "Come to my garden to gather flowers. Come hither."

In the midday the gong sounds at the palace gate.

I know not why they leave their work and linger near my hedge.

The flowers in their hair are pale and faded; the notes are languid in their flutes.

Turn them away I cannot. I call them and say, "The shade is cool under my trees. Come, friends."

At night the crickets chirp in the woods.

Who is it that comes slowly to my door and gently knocks?

I vaguely see the face, not a word is spoken, the stillness of the sky is all around.

Turn away my silent guest I cannot. I look at the face through the dark, and hours of dreams pass by.

我在路边行走，也不知道为什么，

时已过午，竹枝在风中簌簌作响。

横斜的影子伸臂拖住流光的双足。

布谷鸟都唱倦了。

我在路边行走，也不知道为什么。

低垂的树荫盖住水边的茅屋。

有人正忙着工作，她的钏镯在一角放出乐音。

我在茅屋前面站着，我不知道为什么。

曲径穿过一片芥菜田地和几层芒果树林。

它经过村庙和渡头的市集。

我在这茅屋面前停住了，我不知道为什么。

好几年前，三月风吹的一天，春天倦慵地低语，芒果花落在地上。

浪花跳起掠过立在渡头阶沿上的铜瓶。

我想着三月风吹的这一天，我不知道为什么。

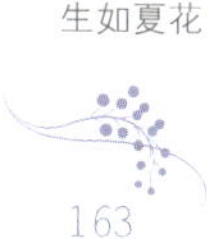



阴影更深，牛群归栏。

冷落的牧场上日色苍白，村人在河边待渡。

我缓步回去，我不知道为什么。

——《园丁集》一四 冰心 译 一九五八年五月《泰戈尔诗选》——

I was walking by the road, I do not know why,

when the noonday was past and bamboo branches rustled in the wind.

The prone shadows with their outstretched arms clung to the feet of the hurrying light.

The koels were weary of their songs.

I was walking by the road, I do not know why.

The hut by the side of the water is shaded by an overhanging tree.

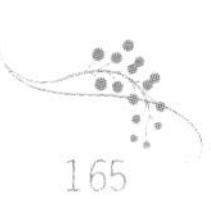



Some one was busy with her work, and her bangles made music in the corner.

I stood before this hut, I know not why.

The narrow winding road crosses many a mustard field, and many a mango forest.

It passes by the temple of the village and the market at the river landing-place.

I stopped by this hut, I do not know why.

Years ago it was a day of breezy March when the murmur of the spring was languorous, and mango blossoms were dropping on the dust.

The rippling water leapt and licked the brass vessel that stood on the landing-step.

I think of that day of breezy March, I do not know why.

Shadows are deepening and cattle returning to their folds.

The light is grey upon the lonely meadows, and the villagers are waiting for the ferry at the bank.

I slowly return upon my steps, I do not know why.

船夫马都（Madhu）底小船泊在赖古尼（Rajgunj）[①]码头。

那是空把黄麻载着，尽管长久无用地摆在那里的。

若果他只要把他的小船借给我，我就要给她添一百个桡手，扬着五个或六个或七个的帆。

我不肯撑着她到那没有趣味的市场去的。

我定要撑她到仙境底七重海十三条河。

但是，母亲，你不要在屋角里为我哭呢。

我不是到森林里去如像那Ramachandra[②]十四年后才回来的。

我要变成故事中底王子，用我喜欢的东西把我的小船装满。

我要携我的朋友阿苏（Ashu）同去。我们要高兴地渡过仙境底七重海十三条河。

我们要在早朝的晨光里出帆。

正午时你在池中洗澡的时候，我们要在外国国王底国中了。

---

①通译为拉琪根琪。
②罗摩犍陀罗，即罗摩。他是印度叙事诗《罗摩衍那》中的主角。为了尊重父亲的诺言和维持弟兄间的友爱，他抛弃了继承王位的权利，和妻子悉多在森林中被放逐了十四年。

我们把提普尼（Tirpurni）[1]滩、把迪本塔（Tepantar）[2]沙滩向我们后边撇着。

我们回来时天会要黑的了，我便要把我见过一切事儿都告诉你呢。

我要渡过仙境底七重（海）十三条河。

——《新月集·水手》郑振铎 译 一九二二年二月——

①通译为特浦尼。
②通译为特潘塔。

## THE SAILOR

The boat of the boatman Madhu is moored at the wharf of Rajgunj.

It is uselessly laden with jute, and has been lying there idle for ever so long.

If he would only lend me his boat, I should man her with a hundred oars, and hoist sails, five or six or seven.

I should never steer her to stupid markets.

I should sail the seven seas and the thirteen rivers of fairyland.

But, mother, you won't weep for me in a corner.

I am not going into the forest like Ramachandra to come back only after fourteen years.

I shall become the prince of the story, and fill my boat with whatever I like.

I shall take my friend Ashu with me. We shall sail merrily across the seven seas and the thirteen rivers of fairyland.

We shall set sail in the early morning light.

When at noontide you are bathing at the pond, we shall be in the land of a strange king.

We shall pass the ford of Tirpurni, and leave behind us the desert of Tepantar.

When we come back it will be getting dark, and I shall tell you of all that we have seen.

I shall cross the seven seas and the thirteen rivers of fairyland.

“到我们这里来吧，青年人，老实告诉我们，为什么你眼里带着疯癫？”

“我不知道我喝了什么野罂粟花酒，使我的眼里带着疯癫。”

“呵，多难为情！”

“好吧，有的人聪明有的人愚拙，有的人细心有的人马虎。有的眼睛会笑，有的眼睛会哭——我的眼睛是带着疯癫的。”

“青年人，你为什么这样凝立在树影下呢？”

“我的脚被我沉重的心压得疲倦了，我就在树影下凝立着。”

“呵，多难为情！”

“好吧，有人一直行进，有人到处留连，有的人是自由的，有的人是锁住的——我的脚被我沉重的心压得疲倦了。”

——《园丁集》二五 冰心 译 一九五八年五月《泰戈尔诗选》——

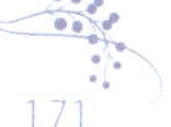



"Come to us, youth, tell us truly why there is madness in your eyes?"

"I know not what wine of wild poppy I have drunk, that there is this madness in my eyes."

"Ah, shame!"

"Well, some are wise and some foolish, some are watchful and some careless. There are eyes that smile and eyes that weep–and madness is in my eyes."

"Youth, why do you stand so still under the shadow of the tree?"

"My feet are languid with the burden of my heart, and I stand still in the shadow."

"Ah, shame!"

"Well, some march on their way and some linger, some are free and some are fettered—and my feet are languid with the burden of my heart."

我在大路灼热的尘土上消磨了一天。

现在，在晚凉中我敲着一座小庙的门。这庙已经荒废倒塌了。

一棵愁苦的菩提树，从破墙的裂缝里伸展出饥饿的爪根。

从前曾有过路人到这里来洗疲乏的脚。

他们在新月的微光中在院里摊开席子，坐着谈论异地的风光。

早起我们精神恢复了，鸟声使他们欢悦，友爱的花儿在道边向他们点首。

但是当我来的时候没有灯在等待我。

只有残留的灯烟熏污的黑迹，像盲人的眼睛，从墙上瞪视着我。

萤虫在涸池边的草里闪烁，竹影在荒芜的小径上摇曳。

我在一天之末做了没有主人的客人。

在我面前的是漫漫的长夜，我疲倦了。

——《园丁集》六四 冰心 译 一九五八年五月《泰戈尔诗选》——

I spent my day on the scorching hot dust of the road.

Now, in the cool of the evening, I knock at the door of the inn. It is deserted and in ruins.

A grim ashath tree spreads its hungry clutching roots through the gaping fissures of the walls.

Days have been when wayfarers came here to wash their weary feet.

They spread their mats in the courtyard in the dim light of the early moon, and sat and talked of strange lands.

They work refreshed in the morning when birds made them glad, and friendly flowers nodded their heads at them from the wayside.

But no lighted lamp awaited me when I came here.

The black smudges of smoke left by many a forgotten evening lamp stare, like blind eyes, from the wall.

Fireflies flit in the bush near the dried-up pond, and bamboo branches fling their shadows on the grass-grown path.

I am the guest of no one at the end of my day.

The long night is before me, and I am tired.

她走的时候，夜间黑漆漆的，他们都睡了。

现在，夜间也是黑漆漆的，我唤她道："回来，我爱；世界都在沉睡；当群星互相凝视的时候，你来一会儿是没有人知道的。"

她走的时候，树木刚在萌芽，春光正幼。

现在花盛开了，我唤道，"回来，我爱。孩子们漫不经心的游戏，把花聚了一块，又把他们散开了。你如走来，拿一朵小花去，没有人会觉得失了他的。"

他们常常游戏的，还在那里游戏，生命如此的浪费。

我静听他们的空谈，便唤道，"回来，我爱，母亲的心里，充满着爱，你如走来，仅仅从她那里接了一个吻，没有人会妒忌的。"

——《新月集·追唤》郑振铎 译 一九二三年九月——

## THE RECALL

The night was dark when she went away, and they slept.

The night is dark now, and I call for her, "Come back, my darling; the world is asleep; and no one would know, if you come for a moment while stars are gazing at stars."

She went away when the trees were in bud and the spring was young.

Now the flowers are in high bloom and I call, "Come back, my darling. The children gather and scatter flowers in reckless sport. And if you come and take one little blossom no one will miss it."

Those that used to play are playing still, so spendthrift is life.

I listen to their chatter and call, "Come back, my darling, for mother's heart is full to the brim with love, and if you come to snatch only one little kiss from her no one will grudge it."

# 孩子·天使

我独自在横跨过田地的路上走着。夕阳像一个守财奴似的，正藏起他的最后的金子。

白昼更加深沉的没入黑暗之中。那已经收割了的孤寂的田地，默默的躺在那里。

天空里突然升起了一个男孩子的尖锐的歌声。他穿过看不见的黑暗，留下他的歌声的辙痕跨过黄昏的静谧。

他的乡村的家坐落在荒凉的土地的边上，在甘蔗田的后面，躲藏在香蕉树，瘦长的槟榔树、椰子树和深绿色的贾克果树的阴影里。

我在星光下独自走着的路上停留了一会，我看见黑沉沉的大地展开在我的面前，用她的手臂拥抱着无量数的家庭。在那些家庭里有着摇篮和床铺，母亲们的心和夜晚的灯，还有年轻轻的生命，他们满心欢乐，却浑然不知这样的欢乐对于世界的价值。

——《新月集·家庭》郑振铎 译 一九五四年十月——

## THE HOME

I paced alone on the road across the field while the sunset was hiding its last gold like a miser.

The daylight sank deeper and deeper into the darkness, and the widowed land, whose harvest had been reaped, lay silent.

Suddenly a boy's shrill voice rose into the sky. He traversed the dark unseen, leaving the track of his song across the hush of the evening.

His village home lay there at the end of the waste land, beyond the sugar-cane field, hidden among the shadows of the banana and the slender areca palm, the cocoa-nut and the dark green jack-fruit tress.

I stopped for a moment in my lonely way under the starlight, and saw spread before me the darkened earth surrounding with her arms countless homes furnished with cradles and beds, mothers' hearts and evening lamps, and young lives glad with a gladness that knows nothing of its value for the world.

她住在玉米地边的山畔，靠近那股嬉笑着流经古树的庄严的阴影的清泉。女人们提罐到这里来装水，过客们在这里谈话休息。她每天随着潺潺的泉韵工作幻想。

有一天，一个陌生人从云中的山上下来；他的头发像醉蛇一样地纷乱。我们惊奇地问，“你是谁？”他不回答，只坐在喧闹的水边沉默地望着她的茅屋。我们吓得心跳，到了夜里我们都回家去了。

第二天早晨，女人们到杉树下的泉边取水，她们发现她茅屋的门开着，但是，她的声音没有了，她的微笑的脸哪里去了呢？空罐立在地上，她屋角的灯，油尽火灭了。没有人晓得在黎明以前，她跑到哪里去了——那个陌生人也不见了。

到了五月，阳光渐强，冰雪化尽，我们坐在泉边哭泣。我们心里想，“她去的地方有泉水么，在这炎热焦渴的天气中，她能到哪里去取水呢？”我们惶恐地对问，“在我们住的山外还有地方么？”

夏天的夜里，微风从南方吹来；我坐在她的空屋里，没有点上的灯仍在那里立着。忽然间那座山峰，像帘幕拉开一样从我眼前消失了。“呵，那是她来了。你好么，我的孩

子？你快乐么？在无遮的天空下，你有个荫凉的地方么？可怜呵，我们的泉水不在这里供你解渴。”

“那边还是那个天空，”她说，“只是不受屏山的遮隔，——也还是那股流泉长成江河，——也还是那片土地伸广变成平原。”“一切都有了，”我叹息说，“只有我们不在。”她含愁地笑着说，“你们是在我的心里。”我醒起听见泉流潺潺，杉树的叶子在夜中沙沙地响着。

——《园丁集》八三 冰心 译 一九五八年五月《泰戈尔诗选》——

She dwelt on the hillside by the edge of a maize-field, near the spring that flows in laughing rills through the solemn shadows of ancient trees. The women came there to fill their jars, and travellers would sit there to rest and talk. She worked and dreamed daily to the tune of the bubbling stream.

One evening the stranger came down from the cloud-hidden peak; his locks were tangled like drowsy snakes. We asked in wonder, “Who are you?” He answered not but sat by the garrulous stream and silently gazed at the hut where she dwelt. Our hearts quaked in fear and we came back home when it was night.

Next morning when the women came to fetch water at the spring by the deodar trees, they found the doors open in her hut, but her voice was gone and where was her smiling face? The empty jar lay on the floor and her lamp had burnt itself out in the corner. No one knew where she had fled to before it was morning—and the stranger had gone.

In the month of May the sun grew strong and the snow melted, and we sat by the spring and wept. We wondered in our mind, "Is there a spring in the land where she has gone and where she can fill her vessel in these hot thirsty days?" And we asked each other in dismay, "Is there a land beyond these hills where we live?"

It was a summer night; the breeze blew from the south; and I sat in her deserted room where the lamp stood still unlit. When suddenly from before my eyes the hills vanished like curtains drawn aside. "Ah, it is she who comes. How are you, my child? Are you happy? But where can you shelter under this open sky? And, alas, our spring is not here to allay your thirst."

"Here is the same sky," she said, "only free from the fencing hills, –this is the same stream grown into a river, –the same earth widened into a plain." "Everything is here," I sighed, "only we are not." She smiled sadly and said. "You are in my heart." I woke up and heard the babbling of the stream and the rustling of the deodars at night.

小孩子们会集在这无边无际的世界的海边。

无限的天穹静止的临于头上，不息的海水在足下汹涌着。小孩子们会集在这无边无际的世界的海边，叫着跳着。

他们拿沙来建筑房屋，拿空贝壳来做游戏。他们把落叶编成了船，微笑的把他们放到广大的深海上。小孩子们在这世界的海边，做他们的游戏。

他们不知道怎样泅水，他们不知道怎样放网。采珠的人为了珠下水，商人在他们的船上航行，小孩子们却只把小圆石聚了又聚。他们不搜求藏宝；他们不知道怎样放网。

海水带着笑掀起波浪，海边也淡淡的闪耀着微笑。致人死命的波涛，对着小孩子们唱无意义的歌曲，很像一个摇动她孩子的摇蓝时的母亲，海水和小孩子们一同游戏，海边也淡淡的闪耀着微笑。

小孩子们会集在这无边无际的海边。狂风暴雨飘游在无辙迹的天空上，航船沉碎在无辙迹的海水里，死正在外面走着，

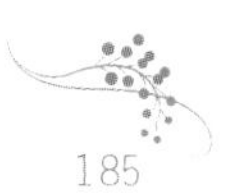

小孩子们却在游戏。在这无边无际的世界的海边上，小孩子们大会集着。

——《新月集·海边》郑振铎 译 一九二三年九月——

ON THE SEASHORE

On the seashore of endless worlds children meet.

The infinite sky is motionless overhead and the restless water is boisterous. On the seashore of endless worlds the children meet with shouts and dances.

They build their houses with sand, and they play with empty shells. With withered leaves they weave their boats and smilingly float them on the vast deep. Children have their play on the seashore of worlds.

They know not how to swim, they know not how to cast nets. Pearl-fishers dive for pearls, merchants sail in their ships, while children gather pebbles and scatter them again. They seek not for hidden treasures, they know not how to cast nets.

The sea surges up with laughter, and pale gleams the smile of the sea-beach. Death-dealing waves sing meaningless ballads to the children, even like a mother while rocking her baby's cradle. The sea plays with children, and pale gleams the smile of the sea beach.

On the seashore of endless worlds children meet. Tempest roams in the pathless sky, ships are wrecked in the trackless water, death is abroad and children play. On the seashore of endless worlds is the great meeting of children.

母亲，光在空中成了灰色了；我不知道这是什么时候。

我的顽耍没有趣儿，所以我回到你这儿来了。是礼拜六，我们的休息日了。

把你的工作停了罢，母亲，坐在这里的窗儿旁边，告诉我那仙话中迪本塔（Tepantar）沙漠是在什么地方。

雨底影子从早到晚的把白天盖了。

猛烈的电光用他的指爪在抓天空。

云彩轰动着，雷响着的时候，我爱的是心里受惊便抱到你。

大雨尽管整时间的在竹叶儿上把打把打地敲，我们的窗儿随着狂风摇的化拉化拉地响的时候。我愿意一个人坐在屋子里，母亲，同着你，听你谈仙话中迪本塔底沙漠。

那是在什么地方，母亲？在什么海底岸上？在什么山底脚下，在什么国王底国中？

那里没有给田野作标记的篱栅，没有通过那儿的路儿，村人在夜间可以走到他们的村庄的，或是妇人在树林里收集下干柴可以担着她的担儿往市场去的。沙地里的黄草就像补缀下的布片儿，只有一根树儿就是又贤惠又老的鸟儿夫妇有她们的巢儿的，迪本塔沙漠是在横着。

我能这样的想像，正是这个样儿的一个阴天，年青的王子单身骑着一匹灰色的马儿经过这沙漠，去寻那王女，那幽禁在无名水底彼岸巨人底宫殿中的。

阴沉沉底雨在远处的空中落着，电光闪起来像是突然发作了急痛一般，他可便想起了他的不幸的母亲，被王弃了的，在打扫牛棚，在拭她的眼泪，正当他骑着经过仙话中迪本塔沙漠的时候？

看，母亲，白天还没完，天早要黑了，那里村路上，也没有行人了。

牧羊的童子早从牧场回了家，人都离了他们的田地去坐在草檐下的席儿上，守着乱涌的云雾。

母亲，我把我的书全都丢在架儿上了——现在莫要叫我做我的功课。

到我长成像我父亲那样大了，我才要学会那一切应该学的呢。

但只是今天，请告诉我，母亲，仙话中迪本塔沙漠是在什么地方呢？

——《新月集·追放者底土地》郑振铎 译 一九二二年二月——

## THE LAND OF THE EXILE

Mother, the light has grown grey in the sky; I do not know what the time is.

There is no fun in my play, so I have come to you. It is Saturday, our holiday.

Leave off your work, mother; sit here by the window and tell me where the desert of Tepantar in the fairy tale is?

The shadow of the rains has covered the day from end to end.

The fierce lightning is scratching the sky with its nails.

When the clouds rumble and it thunders, I love to be afraid in my heart and cling to you.

When the heavy rain patters for hours on the bamboo leaves, and our windows shake and rattle at the gusts of wind, I like to sit alone in the room, mother, with you, and hear you talk about the desert of Tepantar in the fairy tale.

Where is it, mother, on the shore of what sea, at the foot of what hills, in the kingdom of what king?

There are no hedges there to mark the fields, no footpath across it by which the villagers reach their village in the evening, or the woman who gathers dry sticks in the forest can bring her load to the market. With patches of yellow grass in the sand and only one tree where the pair of wise old birds have their nest, lies the desert of Tepantar.

I can imagine how, on just such a cloudy day, the young son of the king is riding alone on a grey horse through the desert, in search of the princess who lies imprisoned in the giant's palace across that unknown water.

When the haze of the rain comes down in the distant sky, and lightning starts up like a sudden fit of pain, does he remember his unhappy mother, abandoned by the king, sweeping the cow-stall and wiping her eyes, while he rides through the desert of Tepantar in the fairy tale?

See, mother, it is almost dark before the day is over, and there are no travellers yonder on the village road.

The shepherd boy has gone home early from the pasture, and men have left their fields to sit on mats under the eaves of their huts, watching the scowling clouds.

Mother, I have left all my books on the shelf–do not ask me to do my lessons now.

When I grow up and am big like my father, I shall

learn all that must be learnt.

But just for today, tell me, mother, where the desert of Tepantar in the fairy tale is?

我是细小的，因为我是一个小孩子。到了我像父亲一样老时，便要变大了。

我的先生要是走来说道："时候晚了，把你的石板，你的书拿来。"

我便要告诉你道，"你不知道我已是同父亲一样大了么？我决不再学什么功课了。"

我的先生便将惊异地说道，"他读书不读书可以随便，因为他是大人了。"

我将自己穿了衣裳，走到众人拥挤的市场里去。

我的叔父要是跑过来说，"你要失路了，我的孩子；让我带了你去罢。"

我便要回答道，"你没有看见么，叔父，我已是同父亲一样大了。我决定要独自一个人到市场里去。"

叔叔便将说道，"是的，他随便到那里去都可以，因为他是大人了。"

当我正把钱给我乳娘时，母亲便要从浴室中出来，因为我是知道怎样用我的钥匙去开银箱的。

母亲将要说道，“你做什么呀，坏孩子？”

我便要告诉她道，“母亲，你不知道我已是同父亲一样大了，我必须给钱给乳娘。”

母亲便将自语道：“他可以随便把钱给他所喜欢给的人，因为他是大人了。”

十一月里放假的时候，父亲将要回家，他以为我还是一个孩子，还为我从城里带了小鞋子，小绸衫来。

我便要说道，“父亲，把这些东西给了哥哥罢，因为我已是同你一样大了。”

爸爸便将想了一想，说道，“他可以随便去买他自己穿的衣裳，因为他是大人了。”

——《新月集·小大人》郑振铎 译 一九二三年九月——

## THE LITTLE BIG MAN

I am small because I am a little child. I shall be big when I am as old as my father is.

My teacher will come and say, “It is late, bring your slate and your books.”

I shall tell him, "Do you not know I am as big as father? And I must not have lessons any more."

My master will wonder and say, "He can leave his books if he likes, for he is grown up."

I shall dress myself and walk to the fair where the crowd is thick.

My uncle will come rushing up to me and say, "You will get lost, my boy; let me carry you."

I shall answer, "Can't you see, uncle, I am as big as father? I must go to the fair alone."

Uncle will say, "Yes, he can go wherever he likes, for he is grown up."

Mother will come from her bath when I am giving money to my nurse, for I shall know how to open the box with my key.

Mother will say, "What are you about, naughty child?"

I shall tell her, "Mother, don't you know, I am as big as father, and I must give silver to my nurse."

Mother will say to herself, "He can give money to whom he likes, for he is grown up."

In the holiday time in October father will come home and, thinking that I am still a baby, will bring for me from the town little shoes and small silken frocks.

I shall say, "Father, give them to my dādā, for I am as big as you are."

Father will think and say, "He can buy his own clothes if he likes, for he is grown up."

母亲，我们想像着我们是旅行，经过一个奇怪的危险的地方。

你乘在一顶轿子里，我便在一匹红马上靠你旁边跑着。

是晚间了，太阳落下去了。约拉迪几（Joradighi）野地在我们前面苍白而灰暗地横着。那土地是又寂寞又荒芜的。

你恐怖着还想着——“我不知道我们来到什么地方了。”

我对你说，“母亲，不要怕。”

草地参差的长着尖头儿的草，一条窄小不平的路儿通过。

广大的野地中不见有牛羊；他们到他们的村栏里去了。

地上天上都黑暗朦胧了，我们不能告诉我们是到什么地方去的。

忽然你悄悄儿地叫着我问我，“近着崖的那是什么光儿呀？”

恰在那个时候那里突然发出一声可怕的呐喊，影子们向我们跑来。

你踞坐在你的轿子里而且把神祇底名儿反复叫着祈祷。

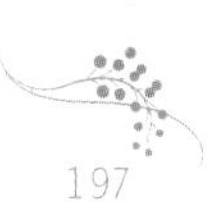



轿夫们，吓地颤着，把他们自己藏在乱蓬蓬的丛莽中。

我对你喊道，“莫要怕，母亲，我在这里。”

长棍子拿在他们的手里而且头发乱披在他们的头上，他们愈来愈近了。

我喊道，“听着！草贼们！多走一步你们就是些死人了。”

他们又是一声惊人的呐喊而且向前猛进。

你捉住我的手儿说，“好孩子，千万避开他们罢。”

我说，“母亲，你只看着我罢。”

于是我放开我的马来狂奔，我的剑同手牌便互相撞的夸拉夸拉地响。

战争来的非常的猛，母亲，你若从你的轿子里看见时，就会给你一个冷噤。

他们许多都逃了，大多数被我寸断了。

我知道你独自一个人儿坐着在想，以为你的孩子必定在这时候死了。

但我染了一身血到你跟前，说道，“母亲，现在战争

停了。”

你出来便吻我，把我紧抱在你的心儿上，而且你私自说，“设使我没有我的男孩子护卫我，我不知道我该怎么呀。”

一千桩无谓的事儿天天发生着，却为什么这样的事就不能偶然间真正来呢?

那要像书中底一个故事。

我的哥哥要说，“有那样的事儿吗? 我常以为他是太软弱了！”

我们村人全都要惊讶地说，“那男孩子同他母亲的事不算是幸运吗? ”

——《新月集·英雄》郑振铎 译 一九二二年二月——

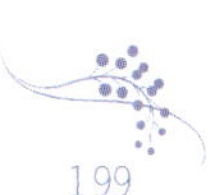

## THE HERO

Mother, let us imagine we are travelling and passing through a strange and dangerous country.

You are riding in a palanquin and I am trotting by you on a red horse.

It is evening and the sun goes down. The waste of Joradighi lies wan and grey before us. The land is desolate and barren.

You are frightened and thinking –"I know not where we have come to."

I say to you, "Mother, do not be afraid."

The meadow is prickly with spiky grass, and through it runs a narrow broken path.

There are no cattle to be seen in the wide field; they have gone to their village stalls.

It grows dark and dim on the land and sky, and we cannot tell where we are going.

Suddenly you call me and ask me in a whisper, "What light is that near the bank?"

Just then there bursts out a fearful yell, and figures come running towards us.

You sit crouched in your palanquin and repeat the names of the gods in prayer.

The bearers, shaking in terror, hide themselves in the thorny bush.

I shout to you, "Don't be afraid, mother, I am here."

With long sticks in their hands and hair all wild about their heads, they come nearer and nearer.

I shout, "Have a care! You villains! One step more and you are dead men."

They give another terrible yell and rush forward.

You clutch my hand and say, "Dear boy, for heaven's sake, keep away from them."

I say, "Mother, just you watch me."

Then I spur my horse for a wild gallop, and my sword and buckler clash against each other.

The fight becomes so fearful, mother, that it would give you a cold shudder could you see it from your palanquin.

Many of them fly, and a great number are cut to pieces.

I know you are thinking, sitting all by yourself, that your boy must be dead by this time.

But I come to you all stained with blood, and say, "Mother, the fight is over now."

You come out and kiss me, pressing me to your heart, and you say to yourself,

"I don't know what I should do if I hadn't my boy to escort me."

A thousand useless things happen day after day, and why couldn't such a thing come true by chance?

It would be like a story in a book.

My brother would say, "Is it possible? I always thought he was so delicate!"

Our village people would all say in amazement, "Was it not lucky that the boy was with his mother?"

流泛在孩子两眼的睡眠，——有谁知道他是从什么地方来的？是的，有个谣传，说他是住在森林荫里，萤火虫朦胧的照着的仙村里，在那个地方挂着两个会幻变的慑怯的蓓蕾。他便是从那个地方来吻着孩子的两眼的。

当孩子睡时，微笑在他唇上浮动着，——有谁知道他是从什么地方生出来的？是的，有个谣传，说，一线新月的幼嫩的清光，触着将消未消的秋云边上，微笑便在那个地方初生在一个浴在清露里的早晨的梦中了。

甜蜜柔嫩的新鲜情景，在孩子的四肢上展放着，——有谁知道他在什么地方藏得这样久？是的，当母亲是一个少女的时候，他已在爱的温柔而沉静的神秘中，潜伏在她的心里。——甜蜜柔嫩的新鲜情景，在孩子的四肢上展放着。

——《新月集·来源》郑振铎 译 一九二三年九月——

## THE SOURCE

The sleep that flits on baby's eyes–does anybody know from where it comes? Yes, there is a rumour that it has its dwelling where, in the fairy village among shadows of the forest dimly lit with glow-worms, there hang two shy buds of enchantment. From there it comes to kiss baby's eyes.

The smile that flickers on baby's lips when he sleeps–does anybody know where it was born? Yes, there is a rumour that a young pale beam of a crescent moon touched the edge of a vanishing autumn cloud, and there the smile was first born in the dream of a dew-washed morning–the smile that flickers on baby's lips when he sleeps.

The sweet, soft freshness that blooms on baby's limbs–does anybody know where it was hidden so long? Yes, when the mother was a young girl it lay pervading her heart in tender and silent mystery of love–the sweet, soft freshness that has bloomed on baby's limbs.

只要孩童是愿意，他此刻便可飞上天去。

他所以不离开我们，并不是没有原故。

他爱把他的头倚在母亲的胸间，就是一刻不见她，也是不行的。

孩童知道所有各种的聪明话，虽然这些话世间的人很少懂得他们的意义。

他所以永不想说，并不是没有原故。

他所要（做）的一件事，就是要去学从母亲的唇里说出来的话。那就是他所以看来这样天真的原故了。

孩童有了一堆黄金与珠子，但他到这个世界上来，却像一个乞丐。

他所以这样假装了来，并不是没有原故。

这个可爱的小小的裸着身体的乞丐所以假装着完全无助的样子，便是想要乞求母亲的爱的资产。

孩童在纤小的新月的世界里，是一切束缚都没有的。

他所以弃了他的自由，并不是没有原故。

他知道有无穷的快乐藏在母亲的心的小小一隅里，被母亲亲爱的手臂所搂所抱，其甜美远胜过自由。

孩童永不知道如何涕哭。他所住的是完全的乐土。

他所以要流泪，并不是没有原故。

虽然他用了可爱的脸儿上的微笑，引逗得他妈妈的热望的心向着他，然而他的因为细故而涕的小哭声却编成了怜与爱的两条带子。

——《新月集·孩童之道》郑振铎 译 一九二三年九月——

## BABY'S WAY

If baby only wanted to, he could fly up to heaven this moment.

It is not for nothing that he does not leave us.

He loves to rest his head on mother's bosom, and cannot ever bear to lose sight of her.

Baby knows all manner of wise words, though few on earth can understand their meaning.

It is not for nothing that he never wants to speak.

The one thing he wants is to learn mother's words from mother's lips. That is why he looks so innocent.

Baby had a heap of gold and pearls, yet he came like a beggar on to this earth.

It is not for nothing he came in such a disguise.

This dear little naked mendicant pretends to be utterly helpless, so that he may beg for mother's wealth of love.

Baby was so free from every tie in the land of the tiny crescent moon.

It was not for nothing he gave up his freedom.

He knows that there is room for endless joy in mother's little corner of a heart, and it is sweeter far than liberty to be caught and pressed in her dear arms.

Baby never knew how to cry. He dwelt in the land of perfect bliss.

It is not for nothing he has chosen to shed tears.

Though with the smile of his dear face he draws mother's yearning heart to him, yet his little cries over tiny troubles weave the double bond of pity and love.

呵，谁给那件小外衫染上颜色的，我的孩子，谁使你的温软的肢体穿上那件红的小外衫的?

你在早晨就跑出来到天井里玩儿，你，跑着就像摇摇欲跌似的。

但是谁给那件小外衫染上颜色的，我的孩子?

什么事叫你大笑起来的，我的小小的命芽儿?

妈妈站在门边，微笑的望着你。

她拍着她的双手，她的手镯叮当的响着，你手里拿着你的竹竿儿在跳舞，活像一个小小的牧童儿。

但是什么事叫你大笑起来的，我的小小的命芽儿?

喔，乞丐，你双手攀搂住妈妈的头颈，要乞讨些什么?

喔，贪得无厌的心，要我把整个世界从天上摘下来，像摘一个果子似的，把他放在你的一双小小的玫瑰色的手掌上么?

喔，乞丐，你要乞讨些什么?

风高兴的带走了你踝铃的叮当。

太阳微笑着，望着你的打扮。

当你睡在你妈妈的臂湾（弯）里时，天空在上面望着你，而早晨蹑手蹑脚的走到你的床跟前，吻着你的双眼。

风高兴的带走了你踝铃的叮当。

仙乡里的梦婆飞过朦胧的天空，向你飞来。

在你妈妈的心头上，那世界母亲，正和你坐在一块儿。

他，向星星奏乐的人，正拿着他的横笛，站在你的窗边。

仙乡里的梦婆飞过朦胧的天空，向你飞来。

——《新月集·不被注意的花饰》郑振铎 译 一九五四年十月——

## THE UNHEEDED PAGEANT

Ah, who was it coloured that little frock, my child, and covered your sweet limbs with that little red tunic?

You have come out in the morning to play in the courtyard, tottering and tumbling as you run.

But who was it coloured that little frock, my child?

What is it makes you laugh, my little life-bud?

Mother smiles at you standing on the threshold.

She claps her hands and her bracelets jingle, and you dance with your bamboo stick in your hand like a tiny little shepherd.

But what is it makes you laugh, my little life-bud?

O, beggar, what do you beg for, clinging to your mother's neck with both your hands?

O, greedy heart, shall I pluck the world like a fruit from the sky to place it on your little rosy palm?

O, beggar, what are you begging for?

The wind carries away in glee the tinkling of your anklet bells.

The sun smiles and watches your toilet.

The sky watches over you when you sleep in your mother's arms, and the morning comes tiptoe to your bed and kisses your eyes.

The wind carries away in glee the tinkling of your anklet bells.

The fairy mistress of dreams is coming towards you, flying through the twilight sky.

The world-mother keeps her seat by you in your

mother's heart.

He who plays his music to the stars is standing at your window with his flute.

And the fairy mistress of dreams is coming towards you, flying through the twilight sky.

谁从孩子的眼里把睡眠偷了去呢？我一定要知道。

母亲把她的水罐捧在腰间，到近村处汲水去了。

这是正午的时候。孩子们游戏的时间已经过去了；池中的鸭子沉默无声。

牧童躺在榕树的荫下睡着了。

白鹤庄重而静定的立在檬果树边的泥泽里。

就在这个时候，偷睡眠者便来了，他从孩子的两眼里捉住睡眠，便飞去了。

当母亲回来时，她看见孩子四肢着地的在屋里爬着。

谁从孩子的眼里把睡眠偷了去呢？我一定要知道。我定要找到她，把她锁起来。

我定要向那个黑洞里张望着，在这个洞里，有一道小泉从圆的和有皱纹的石上滴下来。

我定要在蕾句蓝林中的阴沉沉的树影搜寻去，在这个林里，鸽子在他们住的地方咕咕的叫着，仙女的脚环在繁星满天的静夜里叮当的响着。

我要在黄昏时，向竹林的萧萧的静景里窥望着，在这林

中，萤火虫闪闪的耗费他们的光明，只要遇见一个人，我便要问道，“谁能告诉我偷睡眠者住在什么地方呢？”

谁从孩子的眼里把睡眠偷了去呢？我一定要知道。

只要我能捉住她，怕不会给她一顿好教训！

我要闯入她的巢穴，看她把所有偷来的睡眠藏在什么地方。

我要把他都夺了来，带回家去。

我要把她的双翼缚得紧紧的，把她放在河岸，然后叫她拿一根芦草，在灯心草和睡莲间钓鱼为戏。

当黄昏时，街上已经收了市，村里的孩子们都坐在她母亲的膝上，于是那些夜鸟便讥笑的在她耳边说道：

“你现在还想偷谁的睡眠呢？”

——《新月集·偷睡眠者》郑振铎 译 一九二三年九月——

## SLEEP-STEALER

Who stole sleep from baby's eyes? I must know.

Clasping her pitcher to her waist, mother went to fetch water from the village near by.

It was noon. The children's playtime was over; the

ducks in the pond were silent.

The shepherd boy lay asleep under the shadow of the banyan tree.

The crane stood grave and still in the swamp near the mango grove.

In the meanwhile the Sleep-stealer came and, snatching sleep from baby's eyes, flew away.

When mother came back she found baby travelling the room over on all fours.

Who stole sleep from our baby's eyes? I must know. I must find her and chain her up.

I must look into that dark cave, where, through boulders and scowling stones, trickles a tiny stream.

I must search in the drowsy shade of the bakula grove, where pigeons coo in their corner, and fairies' anklets tinkle in the stillness of starry nights.

In the evening I will peep into the whispering silence of the bamboo forest, where fire-flies squander their light, and will ask every creature I meet, "Can anybody tell me where the Sleep-stealer lives?"

Who stole sleep from baby's eyes? I must know.

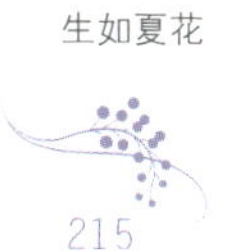



Shouldn't I give her a good lesson if I could only catch her!

I would raid her nest and see where she hoards all her stolen sleep.

I would plunder it all, and carry it home.

I would bind her two wings securely, set her on the bank of the river, and then let her play at fishing with a reed among the rushes and water-lilies.

When the marketing is over in the evening, and the village children sit in their mothers' laps, then the night birds will mockingly din her ears with:

"Whose sleep will you steal now?"

“我从那儿来的？你在那儿拾了我？”宝宝问他的母亲。

她回答了，一半儿叫，一半儿笑，把宝宝搂到她的胸前，——

“你本是同欲望一样藏在我心里的，我的宝贝呀。

你本在我幼时玩的那些假人里；而且当我每早晨用泥做我的神像，那时候，我就把你做了又毁。

你本和我们的家神同龛，我礼拜他时，便在礼拜你。

你住在我一切的希望与一切的爱里，我的生命里，我的母亲底生命里。

你在管理我们的家庭的不灭的精神之膝间养活过多年。

当在女孩子年纪时，我的心心开着，你就如一团香气围绕着他飞扬。

你的柔弱的和软生命开绽在我年青的四肢里，就像在太阳出来以前空中底红光。

天上第一小爱人儿，你是同晨光双生下来，落落在世界底生命流中，最后停泊到我心上。

我一看到你的脸儿，神秘便重压着我；你本是属于一切的便成为我有了。

因为怕把你遗失了，我抱着你紧靠着我的胸儿。是什么魔术竟网罗了世界底宝贝在我这细长的两腕里呢？”

——《新月集·开始》郑振铎 译 一九二二年二月——

## THE BEGINNING

“Where have I come from, where did you pick me up?” the baby asked its mother.

She answered half crying, half laughing, and clasping the baby to her breast–

“You were hidden in my heart as its desire, my darling.

You were in the dolls of my childhood's games; and when with clay I made the image of my god every morning, I made and unmade you then.

You were enshrined with our household deity, in his

worship I worshipped you.

In all my hopes and my loves, in my life, in the life of my mother you have lived.

In the lap of the deathless Spirit who rules our home you have been nursed for ages.

When in girlhood my heart was opening its petals, you hovered as a fragrance about it.

Your tender softness bloomed in my youthful limbs, like a glow in the sky before the sunrise.

Heaven's first darling, twin-born with the morning light, you have floated down the stream of the world's life, and at last you have stranded on my heart.

As I gaze on your face, mystery overwhelms me; you who belong to all have become mine.

For fear of losing you I hold you tight to my breast. What magic has snared the world's treasure in these slender arms of mine?"

当雷云在天上轰响着，六月的大雨落下的时候，

润湿的东风走过荒野，在竹林中吹着口笛。

于是一群一群的花，从无人知道的地方突然走出来，在绿草上狂乐地跳着舞。

母亲，我实在以为那群花是在地下上学的。

他们关了门上课。如果他们想在散学以前出外游戏，他们是要罚先生站壁角的。[①]

雨一来时，他们便放假了。

树枝在林中互相抵触着，绿叶在狂风里萧萧地响着，雷云拍着大手，花孩子们便在那时候穿了紫的，黄的，白的衣，急急的跑了出来。

你要知道，母亲，他们的家是在天上，在群星所住的地方。

你没有看见他们怎样想着要到那儿去么？你不知道他们为什么要那样匆忙么？

我自然能够猜得出他们是对谁扬起双臂来：他们也有母亲同我一样。

——《新月集·花的学校》郑振铎 译 一九二三年九月——

①应为“先生是要罚他们站墙角的”。

## THE FLOWER-SCHOOL

When storm clouds rumble in the sky and June showers come down,

The moist east wind comes marching over the heath to blow its bagpipes among the bamboos.

Then crowds of flowers come out of a sudden, from nobody knows where, and dance upon the grass in wild glee.

Mother, I really think the flowers go to school underground.

They do their lessons with doors shut, and if they want to come out to play before it is time, their master makes them stand in a corner.

When the rains come they have their holidays.

Branches clash together in the forest, and the leaves rustle in the wild wind, the thunder-clouds clap their giant hands and the flower children rush out in dresses of pink and yellow and white.

Do you know, mother, their home is in the sky, where the stars are.

Haven't you seen how eager they are to get there? Don't you know why they are in such a hurry?

Of course, I can guess to whom they raise their arms: they have their mother as I have my own.

# 附录

原来你也在这里
HERE ART THOU

# 太戈尔传[1]

《孩提之天使》

“他们喧哗争斗，他们怀疑失望，他们辩论而不知结果。

“让你的生命到他们当中去，如一线之光，我的孩子，镇定而且纯洁，愉悦他们而使之沉默。

“他们贪望，他们妒忌的时候，是残忍的，他们的话，好像隐存着的刀刃，渴欲饮血。”

“去，去立在他们黑漆漆的心中，我的孩子，把你的和善的眼光堕在他们上面，好像那傍晚的慈善的和平，覆盖着日间的骚扰一样。

“让他们看你的脸，我的孩子，因此能够知道一切事的

①即泰戈尔，《太戈尔传》作者为郑振铎。

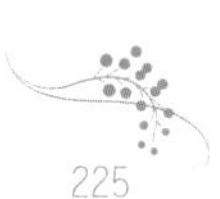



意义；让他们爱你，因此使他们相爱。”

“来，坐在‘无限’的底上，我的孩子。在朝阳出时，开放而抬起你的心像一朵开着的花，在夕阳落时，低下你的头，沉默的完成了一日之崇拜。”

## 一

许多批评家都说，诗人是“人类的儿童”。因为他们都是天真的，和善的。在现代的许多诗人中，太戈尔（Rabindranath Tagore）更是一个“孩提的天使”。他的诗正如这个天真烂漫的天使的脸；看着他，就知道一切事的意义，就感到和平，感到安慰，并且知道真相爱。著《太戈尔的哲学》的S. Radhakrishnan[1]说：太戈尔著作之流行，之能引起全世界人的兴趣，一半在于他思想中的高超的理想主义，一半在于他作品中的文学的庄严与美丽。他的著作在现今尤有特殊的价值；因为这个文明世界自经大战后，已宣告物质主义的破产了。（参阅《太戈尔底哲学》第二页）

---

[1] S.拉达克里希南（Sarvepalli Radhakrishnan,1888—1975），印度现代著名的哲学家、政治家，被称为“东西方比较哲学大师”。

## 二

太戈尔是彭加尔（Bengal）[①]地方的人。

印度是一个“诗的国”，诗就是印度人日常生活的一部分。新生的儿童到了这个世界上所受的一次的祝福，就是用韵文唱的。孩子大了，如做了不好的事，他母亲必定背诵一首小诗告诉他这种行为的不对。在初等学校里，教了字母之后，学生所受的第一课书就是一首诗。许多青年的心里所受的最初的教训就是：“两个伟大的祝福，能消除这个艰苦的世界的恐怖的，就是尝诗的甘露与交好的朋友。”许多印度人做的书也都是用诗的形式来写的；文法的条规，数学的法则，乃至博物学，医学，天文学，化学，物理学，都是如此。结婚的时候，唱的是欢愉之诗；死尸火葬的时候，他们对于死人的最后的说话，也是引用印度的诗篇。

在这个“诗之国”里，产生了这个伟大的诗人太戈尔自然是没有什么奇怪的。

---

①孟加拉。

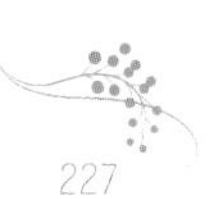



三

太戈尔的生辰是一千八百六十一年五月六日。他的家庭是印度的望族；他的长辈，出了许多望人；他的同辈和晚辈也出了好些哲学家艺术家。他自己曾说道：“我小的时候所得的大利益就是文学与艺术的空气弥漫于我们家里。”他们的接待室里，每天晚上灯都亮着，客人来往不绝。他的兄弟Ganendra在家里搭起戏台，演过Pandit Taskaratna做的戏；他的侄子Jyotiprokash也教过他做诗。他的父亲Dabendranath Tagore更是当时的一个天才。太戈尔在此优越的环境中长成，他的伟大的诗才受了不少的灌溉，自然是要出芽，生枝，而且开花结果。

太戈尔的母亲，死的很早。他在儿童时代，寂寞而不快乐。很少出外——到街上或园林里——去游玩。离了家塾以后，他进了本地的东方学校，师范学校，又进了英国人办的彭加尔学校，又被送到英国去学法律。但是学校里的刻板而无味的生活，他显出十分憎恶。无论到那个学校都不过一年就退学回家。他父亲很知道他的性情，并不强迫他去服从学校里的残酷而不明了儿童个性的教师，只在家里请了人教他。

但他还有两个大教师呢！一个是自然界，一个是平民。太戈尔他自己告诉过我们，自然界就是他的亲爱的同伴，她手里藏了许多东西，要他去猜。太戈尔的猜法真是奇怪！凡是她给他猜的东西，他没有一猜不就中的。这因为他与自然界相处，已久而且很深了。他很小的时候，就爱她；他家里有一棵榕树，他少时常到树下洗澡游玩，到了后来，还记住他：

“绕缠的树根从你枝干上悬下，呵，古老的榕树呀，你日夜不动的站着，好像一个苦行的人在那里忏悔，你还记住那个孩子，他的幻想曾同你的影子一同游戏的吗？”

以后，刚格（Ganges）河[1]的风光，喜马拉野山[2]的景色，几乎无不深深的印在他明澈的心镜里。

他与他父亲的工人，交际得很密切。他在Salaidah地方管理他父亲的农产时，除了Padma（帕德马）河，他的最好的朋友就是一般农民了。所以他竟成了他们内在的精神的表现者。

在太戈尔二十三岁的时候，他与一个女子结了婚。这个婚姻是理想的快乐的结合。到后来小孩子们降临他家的时候，他又得了新的教师了。《新月集》就是在那时写的。在

①即恒河。
②今译喜马拉雅山。

世界文学家里，没有一本诗集比他这个《新月集》描写儿童更好而且更美丽，真切的了。母亲的永久的神秘与美，与孩子之天真，都幽婉地温和地达出了十二分。且看：

“大家都知道你是十分喜欢甜的东西的，——这就是他们所以叫你贪嘴么？

嘻！那末他们把我们喜欢你的人叫做什么呢？”

这句母亲对她孩子说的话是如何诙谐而慈爱呀！总之天真烂漫的儿童世界，教导他以不少的真理。在他三十五岁前后，他的夫人死了。他的爱女，他的爱儿也都相继而夭亡。这个可怕的殷忧笼罩在他身上，使他做出世界上最柔和甜美的情歌，使他的灵魂更有力，更尖锐。他的诗，在这个时期所写的也很优美。后来遂转其笔锋去做颂神之歌，不复作情诗。

“这个蔓延的痛苦，因爱与欲望，更深邃而成为人类家庭里的悲哀与快乐，这就是永远融合，流溢在我诗人心中发出来的歌声中的东西了。”

这是他《颂神诗集》[1]（*Gitanjali*）中的一句，我们读了

---

①即《吉檀迦利》。

觉得他还有余痛浮绕在他笔端呢。

一九〇二年，他创办了一个“和平之院”——山铁尼克当（Shantiniketan）学校——校址在Bolpus离加尔加答[①]不远。在那个地方，他的两个大师——自然界与儿童——已融合在一起了，这个学校的教法，用印度的古法，而参以西方的方术，是一种森林学校。凡是到那里参观过的人都以为太戈尔的计划，非常成功。以前只有二三个学生，到了现在[②]，已经增加到二百人。他得的诺贝尔文学奖金，已捐入此校为基金。听说，他的著作所得的利益也都消耗在这个学校里。Macdonald君做了一篇关于这个“和平之院”的游记，说：“无论什么东西在那个地方都是和平，自然，而且快活。”任何好争斗，好烦恼的成人，一到了这个“和平之院，”听见早晨的儿童的清脆抑扬的歌声，没有不忘记了他的困恼的生的担负的！

他的著作多自己译成英文。最初出版的是《园丁集》。此诗集一出，凡是说英语的民族，与懂得英语的民族，没有

①即加尔各答。
②这里指作者撰写此文的时代，即20世纪20年代。

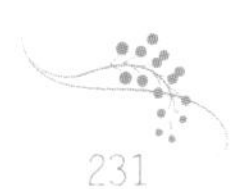



不大大的受了惊骇。以前太戈尔的名字，除印度外，知道的人极少。自此以后，这个白衣的和平天使的威力立刻弥漫于全人类之间，瑞典的文学会，也立刻把一九一三年的诺贝尔文学奖金，致之于他的座前。

一九一五年，他到了日本。受日人极狂热的欢迎。一九二〇年，他到了美国，这个拜金国的国民也是非常鼓舞的去迎接他。一九二一年，他到了德国；德人受欧战之刺激，思想大变，对于这个东方的“自然之子”，更表示一种特别的敬意，据柏林通信说，他讲演的地方，德人特别布成森林的景色，因为大家都知道，太戈尔不仅是“人类的儿童”，且是“自然的儿童”。

在一九二〇（？）[①]年法郎士，巴比塞，罗素，爱伦开诸人在法国巴黎发起了一个“光明团”，为永久和平的，非战的运动，太戈尔也在里边。他又尽力鼓吹印度的独立，曾向英国政府请愿许印度的自治，竟因此被他们把他的“勋爵”（Sir）头衔取消。

---

①实际为一九一九年。

## 四

太戈尔的文学运动开始得极早。在他十四岁的时候，即已开始做剧本。十九岁时，他做了第一篇小说，因此著名。后来继续做了不少的剧本。当时即已在彭加尔及加尔加答各剧场演奏。到了现在，加尔加答还在那里演唱他的戏。

他的著作，初时只传布在家庭内，后来才刊登于（*Cyanankur*）月刊上。他们同他定约，做诗的投稿者。他的散文著作，最初也登载在这个杂志上。

他的著作，最初都是用彭加尔文写的；凡是说彭加尔话的地方，没有人不日日歌诵他的诗歌。后来由他自己及他的朋友陆续译了许多种成英文，诗集有：《园丁集》《新月集》《采果集》《飞鸟集》《*Gitanjali*》（《吉檀迦利》）《爱者之赠与歧道》，剧本有：《牺牲及其他》，《邮局》，《暗室之王》，《春之循环》；论文集有：《生之实现》，《人格》，《国家主义》；杂著有：《我的回忆》，《饿不及其他》，《家庭与世界》等。

在彭加尔文里，据印度人说，他的诗较英文写的尤为美丽。一个印度人对W. B. Yeats[①]说："我每天读太戈尔，读他一行，可以把世上一切的烦恼都忘了。"他自己也说：

"我的歌坐在你的瞳人里。将你的视线，带入万物的心里。

我的歌声，虽因死而沉寂，但是我的诗歌，仍将从你的活着的心里唱将出来。"

是的，太戈尔的歌声虽有时沉寂，但是只要有人类在世上，他的微妙幽婉之诗，仍将永永由生人的心中唱出来的。

他的戏剧和小说，与诗也有同样的感化力。一个印度的批评家说："他的英雄与女英雄都是出于平常人之中的，他们的纯朴的快乱与忧愁，太戈尔用异常的内在的沉刻的情绪，用音乐似的词句，写出来给我们看。"

就是他的论文，也是充溢着诗的趣味与音乐似的词句。他总之是一个诗人。

## 五

"他是我们圣人中的第一个人：不拒绝生命，而能说出

①爱尔兰大诗人叶芝，也译叶慈。

生命之本身的，这就是我们所以爱他的原因了。”

这是一个印度人的话。但我们的意见也是如此：

我们所以爱化[1]，就是因为他是不拒绝生命，而能说出生命之本身的。

本文的参考书

（1）K. Roy: R. Tagore: *The Man and His Poetry.*
（2）R. Tagore: *My Reminiscences.*
（3）C. Martin: *Poets of the Democracy.*
（4）W. B. Yeats: Introduction to “*Gitanjali*”.
（5）“*Crescent Moon*” and Other Poems, by R. Tagore。

①他。

图书在版编目（C I P）数据

原来你也在这里 / (印) 泰戈尔 (Tagore,R.) 著 ;郑振铎, 冰心译. —长沙 : 湖南文艺出版社, 2012.11
书名原文: Here Art Thou
ISBN 978-7-5404-5790-7
Ⅰ. ①原… Ⅱ. ①泰… ②郑… ③冰… Ⅲ. ①诗集 – 印度 – 现代 Ⅳ. ①I351.25

中国版本图书馆CIP数据核字(2012)第228943号

©中南博集天卷文化传媒有限公司。本书版权受法律保护。未经权利人许可，任何人不得以任何方式使用本书包括正文、插图、封面、版式等任何部分内容，违者将受到法律制裁。

上架建议：畅销・诗歌

原来你也在这里

作　　者：[印]罗宾德拉纳特・泰戈尔（Rabindranath Tagore）
译　　者：郑振铎 冰心
出 版 人：刘清华
责任编辑：丁丽丹 刘诗哲
监　　制：张应娜
特约编辑：薛 婷
封面设计：吕彦秋
版式设计：姜利锐
出版发行：湖南文艺出版社
（长沙市雨花区东二环一段508 号 邮编：410014）
网　　址：www.hnwy.net
印　　刷：北京缤索印刷有限公司
经　　销：新华书店
开　　本：880mm × 1270mm 1/32
字　　数：130千字
印　　张：7.5
版　　次：2012年11月第1版
印　　次：2017年7月第8次印刷
书　　号：ISBN 978-7-5404-5790-7
定　　价：28.00元
质量监督电话：010-59096394 团购电话：010-59320018